To: Eva,

7/12/16

This title is a work to reading the "Nativity" almost daily.

Love.

J.J.

RAMPAGE

A Novel

Roy A. Teel Jr.

Rampage

A Novel

Roy A. Teel Jr.

The Iron Eagle Series: Book Nine

An Imprint of Narroway Publishing LLC.

Narroway Publishing LLC.
Imprint: Narroway Press
P.O. Box 1431
Lake Arrowhead, California 92352

First Edition

ISBN: 978-0-9904748-3-8

Teel, Roy A., 1965-
Rampage: A Novel, The Iron Eagle Series: Book Nine /
Roy A. Teel Jr. — 1st ed. — Lake Arrowhead, Calif. Narroway Press
c2016. p.; cm. ISBN: 978-0-9904748-3-8 (Hardcover)

1. Hard-Boiled – Fiction. 2. Police, FBI – Fiction. 3. Murder – Fiction.
4. Serial Killers – Fiction. 5. Mystery – Fiction. 6. Suspense – Fiction.
7. Graphic Violence – Fiction. 8. Graphic Sex – Fiction
I. Title.

Book Editing: Finesse Writing and Editing LLC.
Cover and Book Design: Adan M. Garcia, FSi studio
Author Photo: Z

For those who choose to deal with bullies of all kinds with logic and reason sans violence.

Also by Roy A. Teel Jr.

Nonfiction:

The Way, The Truth, and The Lies: How the Gospels Mislead Christians about Jesus' True Message

Against the Grain: The American Mega-church and its Culture of Control

Fiction:

The Light of Darkness: Dialogues in Death: Collected Short Stories

And God Laughed, A Novel

Fiction Novel Series:

Rise of the Iron Eagle: Book One

Evil and the Details: Book Two

Rome Is Burning: Book Three

Operation Red Alert: Book Four

A Model for Murder: Book Five

Devil's Chair: Book Six

Death's Valley: Book Seven

Cleansing: Book Eight

The act of bullying has not changed; society has. Once limited to the schoolyard, office, or other physical location, the tactics have changed. In today's society, with the World Wide Web and social media, the bully has a litany of manners from which to inflict the greatest harm, and the victims feel helpless to escape it.

— Roy A. Teel Jr.

Why...is the question asked after any mass killing. Why did it happen? In most cases, the why is never answered, only debated and conjectured, while the next... moves through the darkness to yet another unfathomable why.

— Roy A. Teel Jr.

SEAL OF THE IRON EAGLE™

Table of Contents

CHAPTER ONE

"He might want to, but we
won't get that fuckin' lucky."

Los Angeles, California is a sprawling city, covering more than five hundred square miles and has the second largest economy in the United States, ninth in the world. Policing such an immense city and county is quite an undertaking, and Los Angeles County Sheriff Jim O'Brian had been doing it for nearly four decades. Today was no different.

As he sat on top of the bleachers at Rosedo High School and pondered the upcoming November elections that would mark his retirement, the coroner's office and his own team of CSIs, as well as federal law enforcement, processed a high school murder scene below. Jade Morgan called out to him and said, "Jim, you need to come down here. We have a note." He took the last hit off the cigarette he was smoking and threw it over the top of the bleachers into the wash on the other side. He walked down the steps and over to Jade, who was looking at the meat thermometer in the victim's liver.

"So…do you have any idea when the kid was killed?" The stadium lights illuminated the football field where the body had been found, and extra lighting had been brought in since the body was hanging under the bleachers of the stadium. It was half past nine p.m., and Jade said, "He was killed in the last six hours." A yellow tarp hung over the young victim and a second lay on the ground beneath him. Jim looked down at the tarp on the ground and said, "Disemboweled…that's not very original."

"It's a fuckin' kid, Jim, an eighteen-year-old kid. Jesus! Show some compassion." Jim shrugged and asked, "If that's what you called me down here to see, I've already seen it. I was here before you." Jade shook her head as she walked out from under the bleachers and onto the field. She was about to say something when she caught sight of John Swenson's black Chevy Silverado driving in from one of the gate entrances and headed straight for them. The truck was barreling across the field, and Jade asked, "Is he gonna run us down?" Jim looked on, taking a cigarette out of his top left pocket and said, "He might want to, but we won't get that fuckin' lucky."

The Silverado came to a halt a few feet from them, and Special Agent Swenson stepped out of the truck, walked over to them, and asked, "So, what do we have?" Jade shook her head as did Jim and said, "The prom, John. Jim called you, so we can all fuckin' dance together. Jesus Christ! What the fuck do you think we have here?" John looked around at the vans, cop cars, lights, and the yellow tarp on the ground and said, "A murder scene?" Jade kicked him in the shin, and Jim laughed. She drew back her foot and started jumping around. "What the shit, John…are you made of fuckin' steel?" John laughed and said, "No…but my body armor is…ask Jim about the last time he punched me in the stomach."

Jade looked over at Jim, who flipped open his Zippo, lit his cigarette, took a hit off it, and said, "Oops…I should have warned you. Agent Swenson wears body armor under his clothes at all times. Sorry." Jade frowned, and John asked, "So, what do we have?" Jade walked over to the bleachers and the hanging body and pulled out a plastic sandwich bag covered in blood with a white piece of paper inside and said, "It was lodged in the victim's throat. Read it."

John slipped on a pair of latex gloves, took the baggie from her, and pulled out the note. He read it once to himself and then out loud, *"Once it begins, NO ONE WILL STOP IT!"* The note was printed on computer paper in red ink. John put the note back in the baggie and asked, "Do we have a positive ID on the victim?" "Yeah. The kid's name is Brian Donaldson, a senior here." John walked over to the hanging corpse and pulled off the yellow tarp. He took out his tablet and began to process the scene.

Jim and Jade stayed back as he worked, and when he was finished, he walked back out from under the bleachers and asked, "Did you get a jacket from the school on the kid?" Jim nodded and handed him a file folder without saying anything. John read through it and then asked, "Where's the kid's rap sheet?" Jim pulled out his tablet and sent it to him.

John read over the files and said, "This kid was a bad ass. Multiple arrests for fighting, making terrorist threats, beating on his fellow students, possession of a controlled substance with intent to distribute. This kid has had a career in the system, and he just turned eighteen." Jim nodded and said, "Yeah. Best I can get from most people is that there aren't a lot of tears being shed on campus over this guy's death." John nodded, and Jade said, "So, the guy's a bully, and has had a few scrapes with the law. That doesn't mean he deserved to die, especially like this."

John laughed and said, "He's not a kid. He's a thug. He pushed some kid, or kids, too far and got taken out. I agree it was a bad way to die, but hey…we've all seen worse. I'm more concerned with the note." Jim nodded, and Jade said, "Well…that's your fuckin' job. Mine is to deal with this kid's body, do an autopsy, and then deliver that news to the family and the media." Jim laughed and said, "Well, if you want to deliver anything to this kid's family, you will be doing it major long distance because they are all dead." Jade froze for a second and then asked, "How did they die?" The look on her face told Jim and John she didn't want to know, but she had to ask.

Jim laughed and said, "The kid had nothing to do with his family's death. They were killed in the fires three years ago. He was out of state at the time with friends of his family for a vacation and came home an orphan." John looked at the hanging corpse and said, "Well, that would explain his behavior. The kid had PTSD."

"You're now a fuckin' expert on PTSD and can diagnose it on a dead body?" Jade said flippantly. "Nope…it's here in his school file." John looked at Jim and asked, "You going to talk to his friends?" Jim nodded and asked, "You going to look for the kids he bullied?" John nodded. Jade said, "Well…I'm just going to walk over here and see if we can cut down this tortured murdered kid and get his body to the morgue before he starts stinking up the place." Jim laughed and said, "Too late. It smells like shit over there!" Jade stormed off as John and Jim laughed.

Jerry Pinskey was standing under the home team's bleachers on the other side of the field, watching all the commotion. His cell phone buzzed in his pocket, and he answered. "Hey, Tim, what's up?" Tim was with his friends, Alan Marks, Mark Rubio, and Debbie Atwater. "I'm sitting here with everyone wondering why you're not here."

"The cops found Brian's body, and I've been watching." Tim put the phone on speaker and asked, "Do you think it's a good idea to hang around the spot where you just killed someone? Have you ever heard of the killer coming back to the scene of the crime?" "Oh fuck you, Tim. No one knows it was me, and I want to see how they handle this. It's a learning experience. Besides, you all have your own targets to hit before we start the killing." There was silence on the other end of the line as Jerry watched a tall muscle-bound man talking to the sheriff.

Mark chimed in and said, "We know what we are supposed to do, Jerry. You need to get your ass out of there before someone spots you and starts asking questions." "Yeah, yeah…I'm on my way. Are you all at Tim's house?" Tim told him yes, and Jerry asked, "Do you have today's homework? I need to makeup for the work I missed in class."

"Yeah…I have it for you, now get out of there." Jerry hung up the line and walked out from under the bleachers and into the dark parking lot. What he didn't know was that someone saw him.

John had caught the figure out of the corner of his eye and burned the image of the person into his memory. Jim saw the kid walking off as well and asked, "Are you going to go talk to him?" John shook his head. "No…not yet…I have a mental image of him, and I have a feeling we will see him again real soon." Jim shook his head as he walked off the field to his car and said, "School killings are a big deal, John. The note, the kid gutted and hung. This is just a warning of things to come…I've got a pretty bad feeling that this is just the tip of the iceberg as to what's going to happen here." John agreed as he got into his truck and headed out.

CHAPTER TWO

"'The real Internet, the deep web.'"

Debbie Atwater was laying on Tim's bed, looking up at a poster on his bedroom ceiling when Jerry walked in at ten after ten. Tim was on his laptop, typing, as Debbie stared blankly at a nude poster of a *Playboy* centerfold. She said in a monotone voice, "Do you think that I could ever do a layout in *Playboy*?" Jerry was standing in the doorway and heard her say it and said, "Yes! You could do a photo layout, Deb. You've got the body for it, and you're legal. You should look into it." Tim was typing away, ignoring them. Jerry sat down on a chair and asked, "What's up? Are you in the onion?" Tim said, "I'm in TOR now. My old man is still in Afghanistan. He is working to get me more weapons for our attack."

Deb sat up on the bed and asked, "What the hell is the 'onion?'" Jerry said, "The real Internet, the deep web." She looked confused and asked, "The Internet is the Internet, right?"

Jerry and Tim both shook their heads, and Tim spoke without ever looking up. "The Internet that ninety-nine percent of people search only touches about one percent of what's on the World Wide Web. The deep web is a place where you go to get real deals in real time, and no one can track your movements." "Not even the government?" "Not even the government." Jerry said, "It's the super world of trade, and it is what has allowed us to build our arsenal of weapons and also to lay out our plot and manifesto." Debbie sat up and looked at him and asked, "What was it like? I mean…what was it like killing Brian?"

Jerry sat back. His lanky frame stretched across the chair. His eyes were deep set and dark, mostly from lack of sleep. His dark black hair and pale white skin glowed in the light of the bedroom. "Satisfying… scary but satisfying. That fucker has been taunting me for as long as I can remember. He beat me; he ran me out of two schools in the valley. I thought when I got to Rosedo I would be done with him, then he got kicked out of Cleveland High and was right back in my face again."

"Did you kill him outright?" "No…I dropped a barbed plumb from the top of the bleachers on the football field, and it sunk perfectly into his shoulder. I winched him up off the ground using the leverage of a couple of the bleachers with some very strong rope and then tied him off. When I got to him, he was shocked. He wasn't dead and even cursed me and tried to take a swing at me." Tim laughed and said, "Combative fucker. What an asshole." Deb asked, "So what happened?" "I opened him up like a can of tuna, that's what happened. I gutted him with my field knife and watched his guts fall to the ground then watched him die."

Tim stopped typing and asked, "What was that like? I mean…I know you were excited and had adrenaline running in your system, but what was it like to take his life, watch him die?" "It was a little strange at first. It was surreal as if it wasn't me doing it. I felt like I was watching from outside myself." Deb shook her head and said, "Well, you did it, and it's all over the news. Now the LAPD, the Sheriff's department, and the FBI are involved in the case."

"Yeah. I saw an FBI agent talking to the sheriff and the coroner. He was a big mother fucker." Tim looked at him sternly and asked, "Did they see you?" "Fuck no, man. I was out of there after I talked to you. So what do we have in the onion?"

"My old man has some more equipment coming our way in the next week. We really have all the firepower that we need to do the killings, but I figure the more we have the better off we'll be. This is not going to be like those other half-ass school shootings. This is a well-organized paramilitary attack on the assholes that torture us, and when it's over, we will all walk away scot-fucking-free."

Jerry laughed and asked, "What? You don't want to be a pussy like the others and get surrounded and put the gun in your mouth and off yourself, leaving the world with a million questions?" Tim shook his head slowly and deliberately. "No fuckin' way, man. This is going to be as close to a military movement as I can make it. I have been planning this for three years. You guys have only been involved in the last year since we all joined ROTC at school. We have the discipline, and we have the fortitude. It will happen."

Jerry asked, "So, when are you going to take out Rocky Marick?" "There's a party over at Billy Stone's house. His family has a huge home in Reseda, and I have plans for him." Jerry stood up and said, "Well, I'm going to crash here tonight. I hope you don't puss out, man…I can tell you from my firsthand experience if I had not moved quickly, I would have pussed out, and that would have been the end of the plot." Tim went back to his laptop, not giving Jerry's words the time of day.

Santiago's was quiet when John pulled into the parking lot. He saw Jim's car and walked in, knowing right where he would be. He was sitting at his corner table with a beer in one hand and a cigarette behind his right ear. Javier brought John a glass of tonic water and asked if he was hungry. "No thank you, Javier. I will have something at home with Sara." Jim shot him a look as he took a bite out of a sandwich that he was eating.

"Let me guess. It's after ten, and Barbara is in bed, and you don't want to eat alone?" "No…Barbara is not in bed. She is with your wife and her protégé, Karen, and Jade. Those fuckin' women have a girl's night practically every night." John waved to Javier and asked for a BLT, no mayo, with avocado and red onion on toasted wheat bread, with cottage cheese. Javier put in the order, and Jim laughed and said, "So, you don't want to eat alone either." John laughed and said, "I will have a house full of drunken women, with the exception of Karen."

John reached into his coat and pulled out the note from the Donaldson murder scene. He unfolded it, put it on the table in front of him, and read it out loud. *"Once it begins, NO ONE WILL STOP IT!"* Jim took a swig of his beer and said, "What do you think it means?" John took a drink of tonic water and said, "I think that it's part of a much larger manifesto. This is more than just a one off killing of a bully." "So you figure there will be more?" "Yeah…with a grand finale that's going to try to take out as many people as possible." Jim crinkled up his face and said, "What? Like a school massacre?"

John shook his head. "No. Like a school rampage." Jim took a bite of his sandwich and said with a mouth full of food as John's sandwich showed up at the table, "Well, you have no fuckin' way of knowing something like that, and if you start shooting off your mouth about a possible high school rampage and murder spree, you're going to set a whole nation on high alert."

"And what's wrong with that?" Jim started choking on his sandwich as he tried to respond. He grabbed his beer, and John was just about to rescue him when he put his hands in the air to signal he was okay and said, "Jesus fucking Christ, John. You don't see the goddamn problem with that kind of outrageous statement? For Christ sake. In the past several years, school violence has been escalating on all levels and in all grades. You have society on edge. You can't even start to talk about something so fuckin' insane unless you have a hundred percent proof. And second, even if you have proof, you don't take it to the media; you take care of it in house."

Now it was John with the strange look on his face. "Take care of it in house? What does that mean?" "It means that you do your police work, gather your evidence, and raid the home of the person or persons that you have evidence on, then release it to the media. Thwart the attacks." "And if we miss it and it happens?" Jim took another beer from the bucket next to him and said, "It's fuckin' police work, John…you try…I try…that's the best we can do. You start that kind of chatter in the media, and you're not going to stop what you think might happen. You're going to give a lot of unstable people new ideas, and the next thing you know you have a fuckin' nationwide panic, and who knows…killing spree."

John took a bite of his sandwich, nodding his head. "You're right. I'm going to have to go deep web and see if I can learn anything about this note and if there are connections." Jim laughed and said, "Turn it over to your cyber crimes geeks and let them run with the note. It's too fuckin' cryptic. You put those words into a regular web browser, and you're going to get a thousand hits. This is ultra deep web shit. Fuck, man, you will never find this. There is way too much of this shit out there in that arena. It's like looking for a goddamn needle in a haystack."

The two men finished off their food and drinks, and Jim stood up and said, "Well, I'm going over to your place. It's half past eleven, and Barbara is hammered for sure. I'll pick her up, take her home, and maybe get lucky." The two men thanked Javier, who waved at them from his barstool where he was reading the newspaper, as they walked out the door.

It was half past one. Tim and Debbie had taken off in his car headed for Billy Stone's house. He asked, "Are you sure that Rocky will come out for you?" "Yes…he has wanted to get in my pants for a lot of years… I've been playing him for about two weeks. That's why Greta Harold and Beth Sanchez were trying to kick my ass yesterday. Greta has been dating Rocky, and when she found out that I made a play for him it pissed her off. She was even more pissed off when she learned that he wanted to fuck me!" Tim drove down Vanowen Avenue then turned left on Corbin Avenue and parked in an alley two houses down.

"So, how are you going to do this?" he asked. "Billy is out of town." Tim got an angry look on his face and said, "And you knew this and didn't tell me? I wanted to kill two birds with one stone." "I'm sorry. I just found out today. Billy left Rocky the keys, and, according to Rocky, told him to have fun. I told Rocky I would be at the house around two. I'm just going to walk up and knock on the front door." "You're not going to fuck him, right?"

Debbie looked over at Tim and said, "That's my business, Timmy… you and I are friends, but it ends there. We have played around, but you are not my boyfriend, and I'm not your girlfriend. We are friends with benefits, so don't get weird on me now." "How do you know it's not a trap? That fucker could be in there with the rest of the guys and girls waiting to pounce you…then what?" She reached into the back seat of Tim's car and pulled out two weapons that were on the floor, Smith and Wesson nine millimeter M&P Compact hand guns. She took a snub-nosed silencer and put it on the end of the barrel and looked at Tim and asked, "Is this right?" He nodded. She cocked the weapon, putting a bullet into the tube, and then popped out the clip. She put an extra bullet into the clip and said, "One in the tube and ten in the clip. If it's a trap, the only ones getting hurt are Rocky and his friends."

"He's my damn target, Deb!" Tim said angrily. "I have no intentions of using the gun on him. You wanted to know what I would do if it's a trap…well, here is what I'm going to do. If it's not, I will give him head and then ask him to take me for a walk, and you can drop him right here with your own gun." She handed him his gun, which was the same as hers, and said, "You got most of this weaponry off the deep net, right?" Tim nodded.

"Rocky is an asshole, unless you forgot the taunting this afternoon when his thug friends were kicking the shit out of you!" "I remember… just go get him…walk him into the alley, and I will take it from there." Deb opened the car door, and Tim said, "Deb?" She leaned down into the car and had a generous amount of cleavage showing in the ambient light. "Try to get him to take a walk before you start fooling around.

The guy's an asshole, and I've heard that he's a rough fucker with girls." Deb laughed and said, "I've heard that, too. I'm half hoping it's true. It will give me a reason to shoot his dick off."

She closed the car door, and he watched until she disappeared around the corner headed for Corbin and the front of the house. As soon as she was out of sight, he walked to the back of the house and jumped over the block wall into the backyard. There was a swimming pool and two sliding glass doors. The lights were on, and he could see two or three people moving around. He got closer and saw that Rocky indeed was not alone; Greta and Beth were with him, and they were all nude. The lights were low, and Tim was watching and heard low talking and then the doorbell ring. He saw another person head for the door; someone he didn't recognize. The door opened, and Debbie stepped into the house. He heard Greta and Beth screaming her name as they got off the couch and two other people showed up from the other side of the room. And in a fraction of a second, he saw Debbie hit the floor and her clothes being ripped from her body.

CHAPTER THREE

"I remember every FUCKING NIGHT IN MY NIGHTMARES!"

It was half past three a.m., and Tim was sitting on the floor of Rocky's living room with Debbie next to him, staring at six terrified faces. Tim had shot out the sliding glass door, and in the heat of running into the house allowed Debbie to get her weapon before any of the others could get to it. Tim had ordered Rocky and his friends to sit on the floor where he could see their hands. Greta and Beth were softly sobbing…the man who had answered the door had a bullet wound to the neck but was conscious and bleeding on the carpet in front of the couch. The other two men were much older, and Tim didn't know them.

He pointed the gun at Rocky and asked, "So…who are your friends?" Rocky was quiet and in shock. He was just staring into Tim's eyes. He pointed the gun at his head and asked, "Do you want me to put a bullet between your eyes? I asked you a fuckin' question. Who are your goddamn friends?" Rocky whispered. "Um…the guy you shot is my cousin, Robbie, and the other two are friends of his. I don't know their names." Tim said, "You're telling me that you are in the living room getting fucked by these two sluts, and these three guys are just walking around the house, and you don't know them?" Rocky slowly nodded.

"So, it's just a fuckin' coincidence that you invited Debbie here tonight, and Greta and Beth were here as well as these three clowns?" "You killed Brian, didn't you?" Rocky asked in a soft voice. "Nope…I had nothing to do with that. Brian had his own enemy who took care of him. I'm here to take care of you and Billy, but he's gone I'm told." Rocky nodded.

Debbie had gotten her clothes back on and pointed the gun with a firm and steady grip at the two girls. Tim was cold and steady in his speech and said, "Do you see what happens when you push people, Rocky? Do you see what happens when you beat and torture people? They get pissed off and fed up and sooner or later they come after you." Greta looked at him and said, "You fuckin' nerd. You're just too much of a pussy to fight like a man. You have to use a gun, you fuckin' coward."

There was a quiet pop…and Greta's head went back and then forward…a puff of blood and bone sprayed on the white curtains behind her, and she slumped over onto Beth who screamed. Tim looked on as Debbie said, "That's what you get for planning to gang rape me, you bitch. Tim's not the only one who's been pushed too far." Tim stood up and ordered the other three men to face the wall on their knees. Debbie ordered Rocky over to a chair in the corner of the living room, and Tim said, "So, this is your cousin and his friends. I bet they have long rap sheets and that this would not be their first rape party." Tim didn't hesitate. He pulled the trigger on his weapon three quick times, shooting each man in the back of the head.

Rocky started screaming, and Debbie hit him upside his head with the butt of her gun and said, "Shut up, you little bitch. You can dish it out, but you can't take it?" Rocky kept screaming, "Jesus, Jesus…what the fuck are you two doing? You killed people you didn't even fuckin' know. You're out of your fuckin' minds, man. You're both out of your minds." Tim walked over to the chair where Rocky was sitting and told him to spread his legs. He started whimpering and pleading, and Tim screamed,

"SPREAD YOUR GODDAMN LEGS!" Rocky slowly spread his legs, and his cock was shriveled and laying on the seat cushion. Tim laughed and said, "And you've been calling me skinny dick all of these years? Do you remember what you did to me five years ago at Boy Scout camp?"

Debbie looked at Tim with a strange look on her face. "DO YOU REMEMBER?" Tim screamed. "Dude, it was just a hazing, that's all…it was your first sleepover with the scouts. We were just kidding around." "Kidding around…you, Brian, Billy, and Johnny were just kidding around when you stripped me nude and fucked me up the ass all night? That was kidding around? You were kidding around when you held a knife to my throat while you and the guys fucked me one after the other, and you kept telling me, 'Make a sound, and I will cut your throat, mother fucker. If you ever tell anyone about this, I will kill you.'

"Do you remember? I remember. I remember every FUCKING NIGHT IN MY NIGHTMARES! You were the last one to do me as Brian held the knife, and the whole time you're were raping me you kept telling me that you were going to kill me if I talked. You all told me that." Tim pointed the gun at Rocky's cock and shot him in the crotch, blowing his dick and balls off. Rocky howled in pain and fell back against the chair. Beth stared on in shock as Tim looked Rocky in the eye and said, "You will never tell anyone about this!" and shot him in the head. He said, "Let's go," and Debbie didn't flinch. She just shot Beth at point blank range in the head and walked out the back door.

LAPD was on scene at the Stone home at just after seven a.m. They had received a frantic phone call from the housekeeper that there were dead bodies. The large Hispanic woman was sitting off in a corner of the front room shaking and praying in Spanish as she rubbed a rosary.

Jim pulled up on scene along with John. Both had received calls from Jade that they were needed. Jim got out of his car with a cigarette hanging out of his mouth and dressed in street clothes. He called out to John who was walking up to the house. "What the fuck, man… why are we here, and why does Jade want us here?" John shrugged and walked up to the front door with Jim behind him.

Jade was talking to several CSI team members from LAPD and her office when the two men made their appearance. John went to say something but was drowned out by Jim, "What the fuck, Jade? Why the hell am I here at this hour of the morning?" John looked on, awaiting an answer. Jade walked over to the two men and said, "We have a hell of a mess here. Six dead, three shot execution style, two others shot at nearly point blank range, and one kid with his cock blown off and then his head." John looked into the room and took a pair of latex gloves from her and started to walk the scene. The house was small, and the bodies of the victims crowded a small living room and eat-in kitchen area. He pulled out his tablet and began to process the scene, taking fingerprints of each victim and running them through the NCIC. He was surprised to get hits on all but one of them.

Jim was walking the blood-soaked room and said, "Jesus…this was a slaughter." John was standing with his tablet and putting rap sheets with the bodies. He called to Jim and Jade and said, "Pull out your tablets. I will send you over the IDs on these five." John did a few tweaks and then sent over the files remotely. He had put the information into individual file folders, and Jim opened them one by one and shook his head as he looked at the information. "Fuck, John. These three over here have all been in and out of prison for everything from armed robbery to sexual assault." He walked over to where the three men were huddled after their execution and pointed at two of them and said, "These two fuckers just got out of the joint. Home invasion gone wrong?"

John shook his head and said, "Home invasion gone right." Jim looked confused. "I don't get it?" "This was a planned execution, and at least a few of these people were the targets. I think the bulk of those here just happened to be in the wrong place at the wrong time. I think the intended target was the Marick kid. The killers came upon the others while moving to take him out." "Killers? How do you know we have multiple killers?"

John laughed and said, “Take two seconds to look around, and you can see that there was more than one shooter. Whoever did this had a grudge against this Rocky kid. He’s the only one who was really brutalized; he had his junk shot off before he got a bullet to the head.”

Jim looked around and asked, “Okay, Einstein, the Marick kid has a rap sheet but all prior to his turning eighteen, which means he just got a fresh slate three months ago when he turned eighteen. Someone has been holding a grudge.” Jade answered Jim with her back to him as she was looking over the bodies, “Oh yeah…someone had a real hard on for this Rocky kid. I agree with John. This was a planned attack. The others were just in the wrong place at the wrong time, and now they’re dead. But…to be honest…based on these reports, outside of the two girls, the killers did society a favor. These guys were bad people who had done a lot of bad shit. Rape, robbery, kidnapping. The list goes on and on. It looks like the Eagle might have some competition.” Jade had said it half jokingly, and then her face dropped, and she said, “Or the Eagle is going to be hunting for his competition.” John said nothing for a long time and then pulled off his gloves and walked out the front door with Jade and Jim following.

Jim asked, “What the fuck, John? It was a joke about the Eagle.” Jade looked at John and saw a sadness in his eyes that she had never seen before. She asked, “What’s going on, John? I’m sorry. I meant it as a joke. I didn’t mean anything by it.” John walked out into the front yard of the house and stood for a few seconds then said, “We have a very, very, very dangerous situation here…this is something that transcends the Eagle. We have a small group of young adults who are running on raw emotion. They think they are getting revenge or vengeance on people who have wronged them. They have no idea what they are doing.”

Jim took a cigarette out of his top left pocket, lit it, and asked while snapping his Zippo shut, “And you do?” John walked out to his truck with Jade and Jim behind him. Jade said, “You’re scaring me, John…what the hell do you see here that I’m missing?” Jim said nothing. He just took a deep drag off the cigarette, waiting for the response. John put his giant arms on top of his truck and looked at the two of them standing on the opposite side and said, "Hell is coming... this scene is directly related to the killing at Rosedo High School last night. There's a small group of bullied kids that are planning to make the whole of society pay for the sins of the few." Jim said, "You're confusing me...are you saying that there's a plot being hatched by some kid or kids to pull some type of school massacre?"

John looked up at the house and said, "I think there are some kids who think they know what they are planning to do, but they haven't locked on it yet. I think that the attack is in flux while they each deal with their attackers and those who brutalized them. They think they know what they're planning, but those plans could easily get disrupted and even bigger and more terrifying situations could arise." Jade asked, "Another school massacre?" John looked at Jim who was finishing up his cigarette and said, "There is something that has been boiling under the surface for a lot of years here, and it has finally begun to boil over. There will be more killings, and they will be one offs until the personal aspect of the killings is concluded, and then I think that the pathology of these killers will be fixed. They will no longer see humans. They will see cattle, and when that happens, depending on how intelligent our killers are, the situation is going to change from revenge to body counts...high body counts in the hopes of leaving a lasting impression for generations."

Jim threw his hands down at his sides and said, "You're talking in riddles, John. I don't understand what you're saying...we have one note from a crime scene from last night. This scene does not appear to be in any way connected to the school issue. Unless you can make a connection for me, I have to look at this situation as just a matter of some bad people being in the wrong place at the wrong time. It happens every day, my friend, and you know that." John nodded and asked Jade to try and do autopsies on the victims as soon as possible. He asked Jim to see if he could learn who the next of kin was and to let him know if they find any other evidence on the killers.

He jumped into his truck and drove off, headed for the freeway. Jade looked at Jim and said, "I don't know about you, but John just scared the hell out of me!" Jim nodded slowly and said, "Let's have our teams comb through the crime scene carefully. John saw something, but it seems that it has confused him. Let's leave no stone unturned. We have to sort this situation out fast." They shook hands, and Jim walked back to his car and headed for his office.

CHAPTER FOUR

"They hacked my webcam on my laptop two weeks ago."

Sara and Karen had been running like two crazy people trying to keep up with a rush of patients that had been coming into the ER at Northridge Hospital over the past twenty-four hours. Things had gotten a little settled, and the two women walked back to the doctor's lounge and sat down in two plush chairs with a cup of coffee, in silence. Linda Elliott followed them in and poured herself a cup of coffee and said, "WOW! Now, that was a rush. I was supposed to be off shift two hours ago." Sara laughed and said, "Well Linda, you're the only one who seems to take our work and the work of saving lives seriously. Several nurses ended their rotations and left the hospital at the shift change, only you and one other stayed to make sure we had an extra set of hands."

Linda laughed while sitting down on one of the sofas in the lounge and said, "With Gary overseas fighting and Tim fighting his own battles at school, I feel like I'm in a war zone all the time."

Karen looked at the clock in the lounge, and it was a quarter to nine. She asked Linda, "How do you manage your career, raising your son, and dealing with your husband who has been deployed to the Middle East for what…his second tour?" "Fourth…Gary is a full bird colonel in the Marine Corps. He is over there because he keeps agreeing to go in the hopes of getting that all important rank of general. With Gary, war and the corps is an ego trip. He is far out of harm's way, doing what he calls, 'Shining a seat with his ass' work. But he has nearly thirty years in, and there's been talk that his promotion to general is going to happen."

Sara chuckled, drinking her coffee, and said, "When John was in the corps, he just wanted to survive and get out. Don't get me wrong. He loved his duty, and he loves his country...you two will never know how much John loves his country. But he was never looking for the accolades of military life. Rank meant less to him than taking care of his men and the missions he was assigned to." Karen looked at Sara and asked, "John was a Marine?" "Yes ma'am, for nearly ten years. John was what is called a black operative. He did undercover missions all over the world, most of it he can never talk about." Linda sat up and said, "Your husband was a black op?" Sara nodded, and Linda said, "Well, who knows, our husbands could have served together at some point in their careers. Does John stay in touch with any of his old unit?"

Sara smiled and said, "Yes…they don't see as much of each other as they did in years past, but all but one of his old buddies live here in LA, and they hang out every once in a while. John's not much for a lot of friends; he's more of a loner when he's not chasing down the bad guys at his office with the FBI." Linda laughed and said, "Your husband is a hero to a lot of people, Sara. My son, Tim, really looks up to him. He has kept a scrapbook of everything that the great FBI profiler John Swenson has done over the years." Karen laughed and said, "I really never understood John's role in the world until recently. He has made a huge impact on a lot of lives."

Sara was silent for a moment, and Karen also got quiet as Linda looked on and said, "Did Karen say something wrong? John is a great role model." Sara shook her head and told Linda that she was just tired. Linda asked, "I read an article in the paper that the FBI is working with local and state law enforcement on an anti-bullying campaign." "Um…yeah…I really don't know much about it, Linda. It's one of those public service things that the government throws together every now and then." Linda stood up, stretched, and said, "Well, I would love to have him come and speak at Tim's school. My son is not the most popular kid, and he gets a pretty hard time from some of the bullies. Could you ask John if there is a way he could get involved with Tim's high school in Reseda?" Sara told her sure, and the three women left the hospital for home and some much needed sleep.

Jerry Pinskey was sitting in Tim's bedroom when he and Debbie walked in just before eight. "Where the fuck have you two been?" Tim pulled the guns out of a backpack and said, "Eliminating Rocky Marick and friends." Jerry looked at Debbie who was sheet white. "And friends? What the fuck are you talking about, Tim? You were supposed to kill Rocky and Billy."

"Billy wasn't there. He's away with his family. Rocky was, and he's dead." "Well who the hell are these 'friends?'" "We ran into some trouble with the plan…I got Rocky, but he had guests, and they tried to rape Debbie, and when all was said and done between me and Deb we killed six people. Rocky is dead, so I accomplished what I set out to do."

Jerry had a dazed look on his face, "You deviated from the plan and killed more people than you were supposed to? Dude…not cool, not cool at all…you're going to end up getting the cops climbing all over us. Who else did you kill?" Tim was putting a gun away in his closet and said, "I don't know who the fuck they were. They attacked Deb, and I killed them all." Jerry looked at Tim and said, "Not cool, man…

one or two kills in a week, okay, but multiple murders in the same house is going to bring the wrath of God down on us."

Tim laughed and said, "If there's one thing I can tell you for sure is that God has nothing to do with this, Jerry. We started this movement with the goal of punishing those who have wronged us and teaching the general populace a lesson about picking on people. My old man always tells me to stand up for myself, to be strong, and to not back down from a fight."

Jerry was reclining in a zero gravity chair that Tim had and said, "Yeah…well, your old man is over fighting a different type of enemy. He isn't getting his ass kicked and raped and fucked up like we have been our entire lives. Just because we are smarter than the average person doesn't mean that we should be treated the way we have been and continue to be."

Tim put the guns in the false wall in his closet and then walked over to a small computer table and opened a laptop that was on it. He struck a few keystrokes and said, "Read this post on my Inter-friends account." Jerry got up and walked over to the table, and as he did, Debbie sat down in the chair. She hadn't said a word since walking into the room. Jerry looked down and read the note to Tim from an unknown poster. *"Why don't you just die, loser…kill yourself and the world will have one less dweeb in it."*

Jerry laughed and said, "So what's new with that? I get those kinds of posts on my account and my ain't-speak account daily. You know who's sending the messages. It's Brian and his crew…though there are two less of them now. You can't let this shit get to you, man." Debbie spoke and said, "They hacked my webcam on my laptop two weeks ago." Tim and Jerry looked over at Debbie and said, "You never told us about that. What did they get?" She stood up and walked over to the laptop and punched in an IP address, and a whole litany of nude photos came up. She put in her name in the search field, and there on the screen were tons of nudes of Debbie from her bedroom and bathroom. Tim looked at her and asked, "Why the fuck didn't you tell me about this?" "It's not your business… besides, I don't care. Take a closer look at the site."

Jerry and Tim began to navigate it, and as they did Tim's face turned to one of horror. "Oh shit…shit, man…they videotaped the ass fucking they gave to all of us five years ago, Jerry." The two boys watched the video and heard the sounds of the threats and the grunting and crying that they were doing during the scout trip rape. The header on the file had all four boys' names and said, "These faggots liked getting it up the ass!"

Jerry walked away from the laptop and into the middle of the room in silence. Tim was still searching the site and said, "Man, there are hundreds, maybe thousands of videos and still shots of kids and teens on here. How the fuck did they get this up?" Debbie walked back over and typed in a few IP addresses and said, "This is the deep web…this IP is encrypted in the onion of the World Wide Web. You just can't find it with a regular web browser. You have to know how to navigate the deep web." Jerry turned around with rage in his eyes and asked Tim, "Did you blow that fucker's cock off?" Tim nodded. Jerry walked back over and looked at the site and then ran a source code scan in the deep net to try to pick up the site's location.

After a few minutes of hacking, Jerry said, "These assholes made the tape, but they didn't put it up here. They don't have the brains or know how to have set this up. They fed this to someone else, and that person is uploading and managing the site." Debbie walked back to the chair and sat down. She said, "It's a pedophile running this site, and there is no way to find him or her. They just take the smut and post it and then share it with other sickos, so they can get their rocks off."

Tim closed the laptop and asked, "Alan and Mark are probably at school." Jerry nodded and said, "That's where we need to be. If we start missing classes now, it's going to set off warning bells, and we don't want to attract attention." Tim and Debbie nodded, and the three stopped the conversation, showered and dressed, and went to school.

It was just before third period when an assembly was called at the high school. Classes filed into the auditorium, which seated nearly three thousand. Dean Bradshaw, the school principal, was on the stage along with several members of law enforcement and other members of the faculty and staff. Rumors had been running rampant about Brian's murder from the night before and that Rocky Marick had been found killed earlier in the day. Dean stood up before the school and said a few words about the issues. There were a few laughs in the audience from some students and several more who clapped when they heard that Brian and Rocky were dead.

Bradshaw didn't see the humor and said, "While I know that there was a fair amount of our student body that didn't get along with these two students, they are dead, and their families are suffering right now. I have set up for counselors to be here at the school for the next week if anyone needs to talk about their feelings in this troubling time." Instead of the sympathy Dean thought he would see, he noticed a profound sense of ease in the audience. There wasn't a tear in the house, and no one was raising a hand to ask questions.

When the assembly was over, Dean broke off in conversation with some of his senior faculty and said, "I don't know about you, but I get the distinct impression that no one in that building could have given a damn about these two students' murders." Ashley Hines, the head of the school psychology program, chimed in and said, "Most likely, Dean, what we are seeing is a delayed response to the gravity of these murders. Kids don't show their true colors and emotions right away. I'm sure even though these two students weren't popular, over the next several days or weeks, more and more students will reach out for help and try to understand what happened and seek comfort."

Trisha Warren, the head of student services, let out a laugh and said, "These kids are thankful these two thugs are dead. You don't know these two dead students like I knew them. They were rotten. I mean rotten to the core. They both had violent histories and not just for bullying other kids. They had police records that just sealed in the past few months when they turned eighteen. No…I don't think that you're going to see an outpouring of sympathy over these two boys. If anything, what you're going to see is a campuswide state of relief. These two ran in a small tight-knit group of thugs. There are only two of them left alive, John Belk and Billy Stone.

"Those two guys are the worst of the four, and I would venture a guess that they are not in school today as they try to regroup and figure out who did this to their friends and how they can extract their revenge." Dean asked Trisha to would update the school's world-friends page and to put out a condolence to the families of the two slain students. She said she would, and she would send out a message on ain't-speak letting the families know that they were in their thoughts. Dean said, "It's a whole new world with all of this social media. There are no secrets between people anymore, are there?" The two women shook their heads as the group broke off to do their business.

CHAPTER FIVE

"I think we should focus
on killing them all."

All was quiet at Forest Lawn cemetery in Los Angeles. Two workers were cleaning burial placards around the mausoleum. It was the only noise that could be heard amid the hedges and well-groomed lawns. It was half past three p.m., and the workers went about their business unaware that two young men had slipped inside one of the crypts and were sitting silent, waiting for them to move on out of their area. It took a few minutes, but they cleared the area, and Johnny Beck and Billy Stone huddled in a corner of the crypt alongside the coffin of a famous celebrity. The two boys had tablets and had been chatting by keystrokes while the workers tended to the hedges.

When they were alone, Johnny asked, "So, what the hell are we going to do now? Someone has targeted our small group of friends to be killed." Billy was typing away on his tablet as if not listening. Johnny yelled, "Billy, did hear me, man? Some fuckers are out to kill us, asshole…what the fuck?" Billy put down the tablet and said, "Yeah…we are definitely high profile targets. We can't go to the cops because if they find out some of the shit we have done we could be tried as adults. We have to take care of this situation on our own." Johnny asked, "And just how the hell are we supposed to do that? We don't have any idea who killed Brian and Rocky."

"Well, it's going to be hard to narrow down because so many people at school hate us, so rather than narrowing it down I think we should focus on killing them all." Johnny got a confused look on his face and asked, "Are you saying to shoot up the school?" "Do you see another option?" There was a long pause, and Johnny said, "Where the hell would we start, Billy? I mean, you want to kill everyone at school? What if the killers are not from the school? What if they are outsiders who have learned of the things we have done over the years, the things we have not been caught and charged for? Maybe they are the ones doing the killing?"

Billy took his tablet in his hands and typed in some information and handed it to Johnny. He looked down and said, "Well, I guess when you put it this way, there is little doubt that it's someone from the school." What Johnny had pulled up was a video of the meeting of the school about the murders, and there was no one who was in the least upset. Johnny handed the tablet back and asked, "So, how are we going to do it? School isn't safe for us and home isn't safe, so how do we plan to kill everyone when we can't go home or to school?"

"We do it from Rocky's house…only a handful of people knew that he was a trust fund kid. He got his hands on the money when he turned eighteen. He told me that his family was killed when he was a kid, and they left a huge trust fund for him. I have spent a lot of time with him at his house over the past few years. He had a Mexican maid who worked for the family that helped to look after him along with some foster parents, but he dumped them when he turned eighteen and was living back in his folk's home. We can base out of his house. The maid knows me, and she will have no problem with me staying over. She also knows you, so I think that is where we start."

"What about school? If we don't show up, sooner or later they are going to start looking for us. Don't you figure the cops are going to want to talk to us about what happened?" There was a thoughtful look on Billy's face, and he said, "Yeah, you're right. We will have to go back to school tomorrow. I'm sure the cops are going to want to talk to us, but we don't know shit…we can then work to set up a plan to take out the school and the fuckers that are targeting us."

The two slipped out of the cemetery and headed for Rocky's house. They had a lot of work to do and a short time to get it done.

John was looking over photographs from the two crime scenes when his phone buzzed. "Swenson." "I have two weeks off from Quantico before graduation. You need any help?" Chris Mantel's voice was a friendly sound to John's ears. "Well, hell yeah. Where are you?" "Downstairs. They're busting my balls because I'm not real FBI. Can you get me a pass, sir?" John walked down the hall with his cell phone pressed to his ear, speaking to Chris as he got on an elevator and headed for the ground floor. The doors opened, and he could see Chris's towering figure, lean and powerful, standing in a corner being harassed by a few of John's officers.

John called out and said, "Okay…okay, enough already. The man is about to graduate from Quantico, and he will be working in this office in a few short weeks." The men separated, and John walked up and gave Chris a hug and a firm handshake. Together, they walked back to the elevator and up to his office.

John walked in and sat down, and Chris followed. John asked, "You have two weeks off, and you're calling me to do FBI work?" "Yes…I mean, I have nowhere to be, and I thought I could stay at your place and train you like before and work here at the Bureau until I am ready to go back to Virginia for graduation." John smiled and said, "I knew you were a good pick for the Bureau. Of course, you can stay at the house. You're always welcome. I will assign you a temporary ID and weapon. I have a case that I just got into that might be right up your alley."

After a half hour of paperwork, Chris was back in John's office with his new ID and weapon, and John was bringing him up to speed on the school killing and the murders from earlier in the day. The two men sat with their tablets in their hands, talking about the crime scenes when Chris asked, "No witnesses, huh?" "No. At least not officially. I made someone leaving the first murder scene at the high school last night." "The killer?" Chris asked. "If not, then someone who witnessed the killing." Chris looked at the crime scene photos from the school and said, "This was really, really personal. He wanted to see this guy suffer. The note is interesting, too…"

Chris was reading it and said, "I'm not that far out of school. This note was written by someone who had been bullied and tortured by the victim. I would venture a guess that these two murders are just the start of something a whole hell of a lot bigger." John nodded, looking down at his tablet. Chris continued, "You also can't count out the possibility that the guys that these two victims ran with aren't thinking of seeking revenge here either. They may not know who killed their friends, but if there is no outpouring of emotion over their deaths, their friends could do something radical." John said, "School violence?" "At least. Have you put an alert out to the school to beef up security?" asked Chris. John shook his head. "I don't want to send a panic into the school at this point. I mean, there isn't much to go on. We agree that the killings were intentionally brutal and were some type of revenge, but to jump from two homicides to putting a whole school on lockdown is a hell of a step."

"Yeah, that's true, but you also don't want to be known as the FBI agent that could have stopped a massacre but didn't. I think an overabundance of caution is a good idea here. If there is a plot, more security and more police presence will disrupt it, at least briefly. And that might be all the time you need to stop it from happening." John looked on at Chris and said, "You are absolutely right. We might not have a credible threat but better to be safe than sorry. I'm going to call Jim."

John hit speed dial on his cell phone, and he heard Jim scream into the phone, "WHAT, WHAT, WHAT?" John stayed calm and said, “Hey, Jim, do you have a few minutes to meet with me and my protégé at my office to discuss the two recent school murders?”

Jim was standing at the smoker’s bench at his office with his cell phone to his ear. “Let me fuckin’ guess. Chris is in town?” “Yeah.” Jim took a hit off his cigarette and said, “What do you want to talk about?” “Chris has some good ideas on this situation, and I think that we need to raise the DEFCON level at the school for a little while.” Jim took another hit off the smoke and asked, stomping it out, “I see…so you two idiots want to raise the specter of a school shooting or other violence without an ounce of evidence to support it. You do realize that you will start a citywide panic, and every school will follow suit? You do know that it will stretch local law enforcement to the brink and make me put my deputies into the schools. You mother fuckin’ realize that shit rolls downhill, and that it will be my fuckin’ ass on the line for calling this situation out, right? Right? Mother fuckin’, right?”

John laughed and asked, “So what time can you meet me?” “Santiago’s in one hour…” John said okay and went to hang up when Jim called out to him, “Oh, John?” “Yes.” “Go fuck yourself…you need to be up to your ass in alligators sometime instead of sitting on the fucking sidelines making the rest of us take the heat. Remember this, Mr. Feebie, I won’t be the sheriff of LA in a few short months, then who the fuck are you going to get to do your dirty work?” There was silence. Jim hung up the line and stormed back to his office to get his keys and let his staff know he was going to be out for a while.

John hung up, and Chris said, “You look less than happy, John.” “Yeah…well, Jim just brought to my attention something that I had not been considering until this moment.” “What’s that?” John shrugged and stood up and said, “Not important. He wants to meet at Santiago’s, and given his mood and what we are going to ask him to support, we want to do it his way.” Chris got up and asked, “Do you drink when you go to that bar?” “Tonic water, Chris. All I ever drink at the bar is tonic water.” The two men walked out and headed for Santiago’s.

Linda Elliott got home at just a little before noon. She walked in and dropped her purse then sat down on the couch in the living room, exhausted. Her laptop was open on the coffee table, and her computer began to beep, telling her that she had a video call coming in. She reached over and pressed the enter key, and there in front of her was her husband, Gary. A smile broke across her face, and she said, "Are you a sight for sore eyes. Hi baby." "Hi yourself, beautiful…you're the one that's a sight for my sore eyes." "So when are you coming home, honey? You told me three months ago that your tour was about up…then you agreed to stay on longer. Please tell me you're calling because you are coming home soon." Linda had tears in her eyes, and Gary could see them clearly over the web cam.

"Well, I do have some good news on the home front. I just received new orders. I am to fly back to Washington next month. I've been promoted to brigadier general, honey…I finally earned the rank of general." Linda started crying even harder and said through tears, "I am so proud of you, Gary…I am so damn proud of you. Will there be a ceremony?" "Yes…technically I am a brigadier general as of this morning, but the commandant of the corps is going to formally give me my star in Washington next month. I don't have any details yet, but I wanted you to know that we finally made it."

Linda looked into the camera and said, "You made it, Gary, you made it…I had nothing to do with it." "The hell you didn't. Without you at home taking care of things and supporting me, I would never have climbed the chain of command the way that I have. My success is as much to do with you as with me. Is Tim home?" "No, honey, he's at school, but I know he will be really, really excited, and I know he's proud of you, too."

"Did you get the crate I had shipped home a few weeks ago?" Linda smiled and said, "Yes, I did. Well, Tim got it. I was at work, but he gave me the things you sent home. They are lovely, honey, thank you." "I love you, and I want you to have nice things. I have been able to collect a lot of rare artifacts over here, and when I clear them through command I will send them on to you. I'm glad you like them. Did Tim like the stuff I sent him?" Linda looked around and said, "He never mentioned that you sent him anything." "That's teenagers for you. I sent him some military stuff. He likes weapons, and I was able to get him a few trinkets for his military collection. How's he doing in school and ROTC?"

"He's doing okay...he and his small gang of nerds, as he calls them, have been having a hard time of it at school. Just yesterday, he and some of his friends got into a huge fight, and one of them ended up with a broken nose and lacerations. Timmy got beat up pretty good. I wanted to call the school, but he asked me not to. They all asked me not to." The picture was getting grainy and a little broken in the dialogue. She heard Gary say, "You have to let the boys fight their own battles, Linda. It's the only way they build character. When I get home, Tim and I will sit down and work on his fighting skills." Linda sat back on the couch staring at the screen and said, "Fighting is not the answer, Gary. You know that all fighting does is lead to more fighting until eventually someone gets hurt or even killed." "That's why he must learn to fight and defend himself. He's the son of a damn brigadier general, goddamn it, a fighting man. I'll be damned if my son is going to be a pussy."

Linda sat back up and said, "Let's not fight. We get too little time to speak. When will you know about coming home?" "In a few weeks. As soon as I have an itinerary, I will let you know. General Sherman told me that the corps will fly you and Tim and two friends out for the ceremony. I know little else at this point." Linda heard someone calling Gary's name in the background. "Honey, I have to go. Give Tim a hug for me and tell him to get tough. I will talk to him soon. I love you and will video chat with you when I know more." Linda got teary-eyed again and said, "I understand, Gary. I love you, too, and I'm so proud of you. It's just amazing." "Okay, Linda, I'm out." The screen went black, and Linda closed the laptop, laid her head down on the couch, and cried.

It was half past noon, and Karen was sitting in her office with one of her patients in a counseling session. The name plate on the door said it all, 'Dr. Karen A. Faber, MD., Psychiatrist.' She was finishing up with her patient when she received a text message. She saw the look of disapproval on her patient's face upon hearing the phone buzz but didn't say a word other than to continue her conversation. It was twelve thirty p.m., and the session hour was coming to a close. She told the patient that she was making great progress and that she would see her again next week.

Karen saw her out and then went back into her office and tidied up some paperwork and read her message. It was an urgent text from one of her young patients asking to speak to her right away. She picked up her office phone and called back the number in the text. A young female voice answered the phone in a quiet manner. "Hello." "Hello. This Dr. Faber. I'm returning an urgent text. Who am I speaking to?" There was silence, and the female voice said, "My name is Vickie." Karen was confused and said, "Okay, Vickie…the text message I received came from one of my patients. Is she there?" "Not exactly, Doctor Faber. I sent you the text from her phone." The female voice was low and quiet…almost a whisper, as if she were trying to hide from someone. "Who are you? Why do you have my patient's phone, and why on earth are you contacting me?" There was a pause, and the voice responded, "All really good questions. I can't talk right now. Can we make an appointment to meet?"

Karen was getting angry and said, "No, we can't make an appointment to meet. Who are you? What are you doing with my patient's phone? Where is she?" "Again, all good questions, doc, but I'm afraid I'm not in a position to speak about this right now. I borrowed your patient's phone because I knew you would respond to her text. I know you can't talk about her situation. I need to speak to you because she is in danger, grave danger, and I think you are the only person who can help her."

Karen sat for a moment saying nothing then said with a calm voice, "If my patient is in danger, she should call me and make an appointment, and we can talk. I don't know who you are, but if you are worried about her safety, you should call the police and tell them what's going on."

Vickie was silent then said, "I'm her friend. I don't want her to get into more trouble than she already is. She won't talk to you about this, doctor. I know all about what trouble she is in and how much deeper she is prepared to go. Can we meet?" Karen said, "I will agree to meet with you on two conditions. First, that you meet me here in my office at the Northridge Hospital Medical Building, and second, that you keep the conversation to my patient and her situation. I will not talk about her treatment. Are we clear?" "Yes ma'am. What time can you see me?" Karen pulled up her calendar and said, "I have a half hour at three thirty this afternoon. Can you do that?" "Yes…I will be in your office at three thirty. Now, you have to do something for me." "What's that?" "You can't tell anyone including your patient that you met me. Nothing can be said, and it's a matter of my life and my death." Karen was shaken by the revelation. "What you tell me is confidential. I cannot disclose it to anyone. Do you want to tell me something about this secret meeting before we meet?"

"Not over the phone. It's not safe. They could be listening. I've talked too long as it is. I will see you this afternoon." The line went dead before Karen could respond. She hung up the line and sat back in her chair for a few minutes then picked up the phone and called Sara.

CHAPTER SIX

"In this world, there are no do overs, and you are going to learn that mother fuckin' fast."

The sea was choppy and the surf higher than normal. There was a storm brewing just off the coast of Baja, California, and it was sending some very large swells to the Southern Pacific coast. There were a few surfers in the water, but for the most part they were either camped on the beach or on the deck of Santiago's, drinking beer and sharing surf stories. Chris and John arrived to find Jim had beaten them, as usual. He was sitting out on the deck off in a corner by himself. He was smoking a cigarette, and John frowned when he saw him, and Jim said, "Fuck you…Javier made me this little oasis, so I can enjoy a drink and a smoke, asshole. So, what's so goddamn urgent that you would drag me out here? Not that I'm complaining about being here. I'm complaining about our conversation on the phone."

John and Chris sat, and Javier brought John a large tonic water and brought Chris a glass of water. Chris looked up at the old Mexican and smiled and asked, "How do you know I don't want something else?" Javier pointed to John and said, "You might…but you work for him, sí?" Chris nodded. Javier said, "Then I know John…you work for him, you no drink alcohol when working. You want a soft drink?" "Do you have Coke Zero?" Javier let out a loud laugh and looked at John and said, "You grooming this one in your image?" John smiled, and Javier disappeared then reappeared with a can of Coke Zero and a glass with ice. He poured the drink then turned and brushed several of the surf rats away from the men, so they could speak in peace.

Jim took a drink of his beer and asked, "Okay, so we have two murdered kids, a note that makes no sense, and several others with long and brutal rap sheets on ice at the coroner's office. How the fuck do you think we should handle this?" John was looking out at the surf as he responded, "Very, very carefully." Chris chuckled, and Jim looked over at him and asked, "You think this is funny stuff, chuckles? Do you think this is a fuckin' game? This is serious ass shit, Mister 'I want to be an FBI agent.' Let me tell you something, kid. This is the real world. This is not some course at Quantico where if you fuck up you can do it over. This is real life and death shit, and you only get one shot at getting it right. This is not some fuckin' video game where if you fuck up you get a do over as many times as you like. In this world, there are no do overs, and you are going to learn that mother fuckin' fast."

Chris sat silent with his head down as John turned back around and said, "I found some information on some of the kids that the Donaldson kid bullied. There were four names that were prominent in school records and some police reports." Jim took a hit off the beer and asked, "So…what are the names and what kind of police reports?" "There was a temporary restraining order issued against Donaldson filed by a kid named Jerry Pinskey two years ago. Donaldson plead no contest to battery against him, and the judge dismissed the case with a TRO and a stern warning." Jim took another drink of his beer. "Yeah…so how does that put Pinskey at the crime scene? If this kid is such a pussy that he needed a restraining order to keep Donaldson away from him, I think it is very, very unlikely that the same pussy kid is going to kill the guy he took to court."

"There's another kid, Timothy Elliott. He was a part of the complaint as well, and he was protected by the order as well as two others, Alan Marks and Mark Rubio." Jim took a deep hit off his smoke and said, "Well…we have a motive then for any one of these guys. He was a bad ass dude…he was going to get it one way or another. I read the jacket on him, and he was eighteen."

Chris broke his silence and said, "All of these people you mentioned are over eighteen. They are all seniors at Rosedo High School, and they all have the same M.O. They are nerds, class outcasts, who are part of the school's ROTC program. They are computer guys who run in their own tight-knit little group." Jim laughed, taking a drink of his beer and said, "Jesus, you really did do your homework." "Yes, sir. If there's one thing that John and the Bureau have driven into my head over the past year or so it's to read, read, and read. Never take anything for granted. The smallest detail could be the difference between solving a crime and saving a life or losing a suspect and someone getting killed."

Jim started clapping his hands together slowly with the cigarette hanging out of his mouth. "Good for you. You took a line from your boss's playbook." John said, "I think we haul the four of them in and talk to them." Jim nodded, and Chris asked, "What about putting them under surveillance?" Jim laughed and asked, "Based on what? You got a few thousand dollars burning a hole in your pocket, son? That's what you're asking…you're asking the taxpayers, both state and federal, to pay some cops to sit on their ass making overtime pay by watching some kids that we don't have even the slightest proof have done anything wrong!"

John nodded and said, "It's not that easy, Chris. We don't have probable cause to set up surveillance on them, and there is no way that the higher ups would sign off on something like that. We bring the four in for questioning. Depending on what we learn, we move from there." Jim polished off the rest of his beer then stood up, stubbing out his cigarette in the palm of his hand. "Okay, so who's going to pick these guys up?" John looked up at Jim and said, "I think having the FBI pick them up is a little heavy handed. Let's have LAPD pick them up, and then we will watch the interrogation through the one-way glass and see what we think and move from there." Jim nodded and said he would call over to West Valley and talk to Lieutenant Riggs McEllen. "He worked with us on the cop killings last year. He's a good guy. He'll know how to deal with this." The men all agreed and went their separate ways. Jim was dialing his cell phone calling Riggs as he walked to his car.

Debbie Atwater sat on a bench in Reseda park right next door to her high school on a picnic table, throwing scraps of bread and potato chips down for the ducks near the edge of the pond. Tim was off in the distance with Alan, Jerry, and Mark. The four were talking near the edge of the lake out of earshot. She looked over at them and threw some bread on the ground when she heard Vickie Delgato call out to her. She turned to see Vickie walking slowly in her direction.

Vickie was five foot four, buxom, and blond. Debbie sat shaking her head as Vickie approached in a pair of short cutoff jeans that showed off way more of her eighteen-year-old ass than they covered, a belly shirt that allowed the bottoms of her braless breasts to be seen as she walked, as well as her belly button piercing that hung free and sparkled in the afternoon sunlight. While Vickie was thin at only a hundred and twenty pounds, her mediocre face with deep set brown eyes and plain Jane features offset her curvy shape. She sat down next to Debbie and handed her her cell phone.

"Where did you get my cell?" Deb asked. "You left it in first period when you busted out the door with those four over there. What the hell is going on, Deb? We've been friends since kindergarten. What are you into with those geeks?" Debbie got an angry tone to her voice and said, "They are not geeks. They are my friends, and if you can't deal then go away!" Vickie just shook her head as Jerry looked over to see her sitting with Debbie. He smiled at her, and she smiled back, batting her brown eyes and making a kissing gesture. Debbie looked at her and asked, "What the fuck are you doing?" "Saying hi." "No, you're not. You're being a tease. You hate Jerry. You have gone out of your way to treat him like shit since you got those damn tits three years ago." Vickie laughed and said, "Well, I think that he's handsome, and I have seen a more masculine side of him over the past few weeks." Debbie just shook her head and said, "Yeah whatever…thanks for bringing me my phone. I didn't realize I left it. I'm a little scattered today."

"I noticed. I also know that Jerry and Timmy are into some bad shit, Deb. I hope you're not involved." Debbie looked over at Vickie and asked, "What are you talking about?" Vickie took some of the crumbs from her and started throwing them to the now quacking ducks. "You know exactly what I'm talking about. Jerry told me all about it before he came to the school to get Brian the other night." Deb sat silent, staring at the water. "Oh, don't play dumb with me. I know you and what Jerry did to Brian." Debbie sat silent, throwing the remaining crumbs to the ducks then stood up and walked to the water's edge with Vickie hot on her heels.

"It's not that Brian didn't have it coming for God's sake. He was a mean ass mother fucker who was no good…the last time I let him fuck me, he told me how great it was to be eighteen and to have his childhood sealed in the eyes of the law," Vickie said as Debbie stared out over the water.

"So…what…he was going to turn over a new leaf? He was going to be a better person now that he was an adult, Vick? Is that what I'm to believe?" Vickie laughed and said, "Oh, hell no…he had all kinds of bad ass plans for keeping up the same behavior and worse. I hated the fuckin' guy, Deb." Debbie laughed and said, "Yeah, you hated him…yet you fucked him every chance you got." Vickie laughed and said, "Yes, yes I did. I let that fucker fuck me anyway he wanted, and you know why?" Debbie just shook her head slowly. "Because I'm not pretty like you. Because I'm not popular…when I started seeing Brian the hate messages and ugly posts stopped on the boards. Because I was popular despite my plain looks." Debbie looked at her and said, "You have that body…and you don't miss a chance to use that. You don't get it, do you Vickie? You would be popular no matter who you were with. You're hot. You have a great body, and every guy in school wants into those tight ass jeans. You didn't have to take Brian's abuse to stop the cyber-bullying or the bullying at school. All you have to do is be yourself. Shit…if you didn't put out as much as you do, you would probably be even more popular because all the boys would be clamoring to get into your pants, so no one would want to make you angry or say or message bad things about you."

Vickie looked thoughtfully as Debbie spoke, and when she had finished Vickie said, "I had never thought of it like that. I will have to give it a try and see what happens. But you changed the subject. What do you know of further plans from those four outside of what Jerry did to Brian?" "No comment!" Vickie threw her head back and said, "Jesus…for a chick with a genius IQ you can be dense. You don't get it. You're in this shit. I'm your friend. I'm trying to save you." Debbie looked down into the sparkling water and said, "It's too late, Vickie…it's just way too late for saving me. You are better off getting the hell away from Jerry and the rest of us."

Vickie stood for a moment looking at Debbie then huffed and turned to walk away. She was headed for a small bridge that connected the park from the street next to the school, and Debbie watched her walking away and then ran after her. She caught Vickie at the edge of the bridge and said out of breath, "School…school…homecoming is in the next week. Are you going?" Vickie nodded. "DON'T!" Vickie's face dropped as she looked into Debbie's tired eyes. "Why not?" "Don't ask me questions you know I can't answer. Just don't come to homecoming. Stay as far away from the dance and the whole thing as you can…okay?" Vickie shivered and Debbie saw it. Vickie looked her straight in the eyes and asked, "Will something bad happen to me if I go to homecoming?" Debbie looked away and said, "I don't know…if you truly are my friend just listen to me and stay away."

Vickie reached out and hugged Debbie and said, "Okay, okay, whatever you say, Deb, whatever you say." Vickie walked across the bridge and on to school. Debbie watched her until she disappeared between bushes and buildings, and she leaned against the concrete bridge and started to cry.

Tim had been watching the girls talking while Jerry was ranting on and on about the deep web and the cell sites he was able to access to pull down more and more information for their plan. Tim pulled himself back into the conversation and asked, "How deep are we in the web?" "Deep, brother. Really mother fuckin' deep. It's all encrypted shit, man. I've been writing code in there for years. None of this pop culture social web for us, man. We are leaving our message to the world with our actions, not on social media in the one percent web world."

Tim looked at Alan and Mark and asked, "Where are you two in the planning? Are you in the deep web, too?" They both nodded, and Mark said, "We have a lot of support, man, a lot of support. There are so many of us out there all over the world fed up with the cliques and the school bullshit. It's really cool when I log into the chat rooms and talk. People are not just listening…man. Tim, they understand…they understand what we have been and are going through and support us a hundred percent. It's love, man; it's pure love."

Mark was tearing up, and Tim and Jerry looked at him, and Jerry said, "Dude…we know you're gay…we know you liked the ass fucking you got from Rocky and Brian and the rest of those fuckers at camp. We didn't, and two of those fuckers are dead. Now, you want to turn your attention to your homo lover target, who, last month, first pissed and shit in one of the school toilets along with Rocky, Brian, Johnny, and Billy then ripped off your pants and underwear, bent you over the bowl, shoved your face into their shit, and raped you with ten different bottles and pipes?"

Mark started to tear up again but with the tears came a look of rage. "Those fuckers…Jesus Christ. I was in the hospital for two weeks." "You remember it, Mark? Remember when Tim and I walked into the bathroom?" Mark nodded. Tim said, "And there protecting the door was Coach Hameln and Coach Dell while those fuckers did that to you." Mark nodded slowly and said, "I'm their star running back, and Hameln just laughed as did Dell. I remember hearing them both taunting those fuckers, 'Give it to him hard, boys…he likes it hard.' Fuckin' Dell was there watching, and he has fucked me at least fifty times in the past three years. He told me later that he couldn't step in and stop it. He said if he did then they would know he was gay and that he loved me."

Jerry said, "Well, you have some targets here, and we don't want them alive for the rest of our event, so what are you going to do about it?" "I'm having dinner at Brad Dell's house tonight. Now that my ass is healed he wants to 'get him some of that' as he said to me this morning, and I will kill him in his sleep." Tim handed Mark a field knife that he got from his father and said, "This fucker can practically field dress an animal with the slightest touch…it will kill real good for you." Jerry said, "Okay…so Mark takes out Dell tonight. I'm going to take out Hameln, and Tim, you're going to take out Johnny." There were head nods all around, and as they were preparing to part, Debbie walked into the middle of the four.

She had heard enough to know what they had planned and said, "That's too many killings for one night. If you do it, the cops will know right away that there is a much larger plot afoot, and we will all get caught." Jerry pushed her and asked, "So what do you want us to do, just sit on our hands? We have a plan." Tim pushed Jerry and said, "Don't you ever treat Debbie like that again. She is only looking out for all of us, you asshole." Debbie had no reaction. She just looked at Tim and said, "It's true, Timmy…you know that what I'm saying is true." Tim nodded and said, "Jerry, stay the fuck home. Do more of your deep web shit and post more of our manifesto. There's still a lot that you need to put up on the plan, so others can follow in our footsteps. Debbie is going to stay with me at my place tonight, so we have alibis in the event we need one.

"Look, Mark, you take out Dell tonight, but don't let anyone see you at his house." Mark started laughing, "The fucker's the assistant coach of the varsity football team. He's in the fuckin' closet. Do you think that he and I have been carrying on for years at his house in plain sight? Shit, man, you don't know the lengths that closet fags go to to keep their secrets. No one has ever seen me with him, and no one ever will. I will, however, make sure that I leave a bloody and fucked up crime scene that shows he's a closet fag, and that he got killed by a jealous male lover."

Tim laughed and asked, "And just how the fuck are you going to do that?" "Coach Dell doesn't know it yet…but his wife got a text from his phone, telling her to be home at ten p.m., that her man has a special surprise for her." Jerry and Tim started laughing as did Alan and Debbie. Alan said…"You didn't?" Mark nodded emphatically, "Oh, but I did…I grabbed Dell's cell while he was in the gym and sent that bitch a text. She is going to walk in while he's pounding away on my sweet, tight, eighteen year-old ass, and there's a shotgun that Dell keeps next to the dresser in his bedroom that is next to the door, and Mrs. Dell is going to grab that fucker and blow his balls off before she gets her throat slit by the jealous other man."

Tim asked, "And you have the clothing and other belongings to leave behind from the 'killer?'" Mark nodded slowly. Debbie asked, "And who is the killer supposed to be?" Mark started laughing and said, "His secret lover, Coach Trent Hameln." The whole group broke out into laughter as they started to walk back to the school and into the battle zone.

Margo Dell was typing away on her keyboard at her law office when she got a text from her husband, Brad, about a surprise for her later that night. She smiled and put her cell phone back on her desk as she continued to type on the brief that was due in court for Judge Larry Robinson in a case she had been assigned as a public defender. She was typing like crazy, trying to get the brief completed, so she could leave the office before midnight for the first time in several weeks. She was excitedly humming and said to herself, "I hope he makes the garlic chicken. It's so great."

CHAPTER SEVEN

"She's just a casualty of war,
babe. Collateral damage."

Sara had just finished her rounds when she got a page from Karen that she needed her, but she had been too busy to respond timely. Sara pulled some charts from one of the nurse's stations and put the cup of coffee she was drinking from one of the ER vending machines between her teeth to hold as her hands were full and walked to the elevator to head for Karen's office. Sara had her medical records computer in her hands, and she was reading an electronic chart while waiting for the elevator. She looked down at her watch, and it was twenty after three. Sara was so into her log computer and other things that she didn't notice the buxom blond girl standing next to her waiting for the elevator as well. The two entered, and Sara stood with the cup clinched between her teeth reading as Vickie Delgato asked, "What floor, Doctor?"

Sara looked down to see Vickie's bright eyes beaming back at her and said, "Five, please," with the paper cup still in her mouth. Vickie pressed the button and said, "That's where I'm going, too, and you must have office hours up there?" Sara laughed into her cup and said through its echo, "No. A colleague of mine has buzzed me for a consult." The elevator opened, and Sara walked on to Karen's office with her little friend right next to her. Sara wasn't paying attention, and she heard the ring of a cell phone, and the girl stopped and stepped off into a corner of the hall. Sara shrugged and kicked the outside of Karen's office door until Karen answered it.

"Oh for crying out loud, Sara. You're not a damn circus performer. You look like a trained seal." Sara laughed as Karen took some of the files out of her hands, and she was able to take the cup out of her mouth and said, "Well, there are times when I sure as hell feel like one." Karen laughed and walked Sara back to her office.

Vickie was standing in a corner two doors down from Karen's office talking quietly on the phone. "You have the night free? I thought you had things to do tonight?" Jerry Pinskey was standing in the student parking lot at the high school off in a corner away from eyes and ears as he spoke to Vickie. "Well, I don't have a free night. I have some homework, but outside of that I'm horny. You want to come over and fool around?" Vickie sighed into the phone, "Is that all it's ever going to be, Jerry? I come over, and you get your rocks off in me, and then I sit and watch you play one of your stupid video games or work on your laptop? I want some romance. At least take me out for dinner." "Okay. Where do you want to go?" "Um… somewhere romantic!" she said with excitement.

"I don't do romantic. We are not a romance, Vickie. You fill my needs, and I fill yours." "Yeah, well, you haven't been keeping up with fulfilling my needs sexually lately, so if I'm going to get fucked I at least want a nice meal." Jerry was curt, "Fine. Where?" "Brown's Place." Jerry's face got red as he yelled into the phone, "Brown's Place…Jesus, Vickie, that place is expensive." "Well, so are my assets…and you know exactly what I mean. I give you all those porno fantasies that you want to fulfill with my body. You can buy me a nice damn meal, Jerry, unless…" There was a pregnant pause before she continued, "you just want straight vanilla missionary sex with no other holes in play."

Jerry pulled the phone close to his lips and said in a whisper, "So, I take you to Brown's Place, and I get to do whatever I want to you?" "You got it, big boy…within limits…I don't mind the bondage stuff, but I don't want you to hurt me like you did a few months ago with those whips…what's the sense in having a safe word if your partner isn't going to listen?" Jerry had a raging erection, and he looked down to see his pulse in his jeans. "I will recognize your safe word. I will do anything you want. A romantic dinner, it is. Money is no object." Vickie laughed and asked, "Are you going to have Tim, Alan, and Mark over to play? I know how obsessed you are with thinking that you can swing Mark straight with straight sex, but it isn't working. He did me once, and it was in the ass and in the dark, and I couldn't say anything. He told me he was fantasizing about you."

Jerry got pissed off and said, "He didn't fuckin' say that, and you know it. He told me he enjoyed the sex with you. You're just trying to piss me off." Vickie laughed and told him that he caught her. She asked, "So, will the guys be with us?" "No…Tim is hanging out with Debbie, and Alan has some homework to do as well, but he's doing it alone, and Mark…well Mark has a date with his boyfriend." Vickie laughed and said, "He's going back to fuckin' Dell after what he and Hameln helped the others do to him?" "Well, yes and no…there's going to be a touch of revenge…okay… a shit load of hardcore revenge."

"Like what you did to Brian?" "Oh no. What he's going to do to Dell makes what I did to Brian look like candy land." Vickie looked around the office corridor and asked, "When is he doing it?" "Tonight about ten. That's why I need you. I need an alibi, and if I get you fed early, I can be fuckin' you while he's fucking up Dell and his wife." "What does Coach Dell's wife, Margo, have to do with anything? She hasn't done anything wrong."

"She's just a casualty of war, babe. Collateral damage." Vickie was quiet for a few seconds and then said, "Pick me up at home at six." "What time is it now?" he asked. "Three thirty-five." "Okay, I will see you then." Jerry hung up and started back across the student parking lot for classes. Vickie hung up and looked down at the phone and then the floor and then Karen's office door. She whispered to herself, "I have to have someone I can talk to. I can't keep this all in. This doctor has to help me and Debbie and maybe save Mark and Margo." She walked down the hall and knocked on Karen's door.

Jim was sitting in his office with two other deputies, giving them instructions with regard to picking up Jerry, Alan, Mark, and Tim for questioning in the Donaldson murder. He had decided to do it himself rather than have LAPD involved. It was quarter to four when the two deputies left to pick up the boys, and Jim called John and said, "Okay…so I'm the bad guy here. I sent two of my high ranking deputies out to pick up the kids. What do you want to tell the parents when they come flying in after us?"

"The truth. They are persons of interest in a homicide." John's voice resonated over the speakerphone, and Jim slammed his fist down on his desk and yelled, "They are not persons of interest in a fuckin' homicide, you dumbass. They are persons of interest to you, to the FBI, not to me…so when these boys get picked up and brought in, you and your protégé better be prepared to be in my office for the interrogation."

"We will be. We will be watching you work your magic from the other side of the one way glass." "Fuck you, John…shit, fuck you!" Jim slammed his fist down on the office phone sending it to the floor and getting a look of disapproval from his office staff outside the open office door. He walked over to the window, picked up the pack of cigarettes, and plopped one into his left hand. He put it in his mouth, lit it, and stood blowing the smoke out the window, muttering to himself.

There was a light tap on Karen's office door, and Sara, being closer to it than Karen, opened it to see Vickie Delgato standing in the doorway. Sara invited her in. Karen was sitting at her desk and stood up to greet the teen. Vickie looked at the two women and put her hand out to Sara and said, "I'm Vickie Delgato, Dr. Faber. We spoke on the phone earlier." A smile broke out across Sara's face, and she said, "My name is Dr. Swenson, Vickie. Dr. Faber is the one standing behind the desk." Vickie looked hard at Karen and said, "You're a doctor?" Karen nodded slowly, and Vickie blurted out, "How the hell old are you?"

Karen walked around her desk and reached out her hand in a gesture to shake hands and said, "I don't know that that is really your business at this moment, Ms. Delgato. You called me from my patient's cell phone, telling me she is in danger and asking to speak to me. I think before we go much farther I need to get an understanding of who you are and what you are doing here." Sara excused herself, but Karen asked her to stay. She pointed to an over-stuffed leather chair in a corner of her office and asked Vickie to sit. Sara took a seat opposite Vickie, and Karen sat down in an office chair that she used for patient sessions.

Vickie sat down, and Karen pulled out a tablet and asked, "So... Ms. Delgato, what is the emergency that you seem to so urgently need to speak to me about that pertains to my patient?" Vickie looked at Sara and let out a little laugh and asked, "Is she really a doctor? A psychiatrist?" Sara nodded, and Vickie said, "But, but...she can't be much older than me." Karen asked, "How old are you, Ms. Delgato?" "Eighteen, two months ago." Karen smiled and said, "I turned eighteen a few weeks ago. I am a doctor, and I'm a board certified psychiatrist. Now, how can I help you?" Vickie sat back in the chair, her breasts busting out of her skimpy top.

She said, "My friend is in trouble." "Your friend Debbie Atwater?" She nodded. "What kind of trouble?" Vickie squirmed a little in her seat, and Sara asked, "Would you like us to refer you to another doctor? Dr. Faber could have a conflict here as she cannot treat you and your friend." "I'm not here for treatment. I'm here to see if this 'doctor' that Debbie has told me so much about can help to save her from prison and possibly death." Sara sat back, and Karen said, "I don't know. What's the crisis? What is going on with Debbie? You mentioned prison, so it's not health related, is it?"

"It will be if she keeps going down the road she's heading down." Vickie went to stand, and Karen said, "Where are you going?" "I made a mistake. I should never have called you. I should never have come here. I need the police. I need to talk to the police." She was only partially up and then fell back in the chair and began to cry. Sara asked, "Why do you need the police? You need to give us more information if we are going to guide you in the right direction either way." Vickie sat sobbing and said, "People are going to die. People have already died. It's going to get worse, much worse." Karen asked, "Who has died?"

"Brian Donaldson." "And who is Brian Donaldson?" Karen asked. Sara chimed in and asked Vickie, "Brian Donaldson who was found murdered at Rosedo High School the other night?" Vickie nodded. "Do you know who killed him?" Vicki nodded again. Sara looked at Karen and then asked Vickie, "Did your friend, Debbie, kill Brian?" Vickie got an indignant look on her face and said, "No…she had nothing to do with his death." Karen asked, "But you know who did kill him?" Vickie nodded and said, "Yeah…yeah, I know."

Karen said, "This is a matter for the police. We need to contact them immediately." Karen stood up, and Vickie cried out, "Wait… there is another murder that's going to happen tonight, and I know the kid who thinks he's going to commit it, but most likely in the end is going to be the victim." Sara said, "Before you say anything more, I want you to sit still. You are talking about criminal offenses that you claim to have knowledge of. Those admissions are not protected by doctor-patient confidentiality. Dr. Faber and I are required by law to notify law enforcement immediately." "The cops can't save anyone. It's too late. Things are happening right now even as we speak."

Sara asked, "What's happening?" "I don't know the details. All I know is that Brian is dead, and so are Rocky and his friends as well as two of my girls friends from school. Debbie has warned me to stay away from school for homecoming, and one of my friends who's gay and has been the victim of some cruel people is going to end up being brutalized again because he thinks he has all of the answers." Sara stood up and pulled out her cell phone. Karen sat still and asked Vickie to do the same. She looked at Karen and asked, "Who is she calling?" "Her husband, I imagine. He is an FBI agent. If anyone can sort out what you know, it's him." Vickie started to hyperventilate and said, "Oh God…Oh God…they are going to kill ME! If they find out what I've done, they will kill me." Sara had the phone to her ear, and she looked at Vickie and said in a firm yet soothing voice, "No one is going to kill you…the man I'm calling will make sure of that."

John's cell phone was ringing on the other end of the line as Sara spoke. "Swenson." "Honey…I need you here at the hospital immediately. We have a young woman in Karen's office who claims she knows about a lot of things that have happened in the last forty-eight hours, namely who killed Brian Donaldson." "I'm on my way. Don't let her leave." "No problem." Sara hung up the line and looked at her watch. It was half past five.

"You are going to stay here with me and Dr. Faber until my husband gets here. He will take care of you from there." "Who is your husband?" "He is the head of the FBI here in Los Angeles, and he will protect you. However, you will have to tell him everything that you know about the killings and any other plots to kill others." Vickie nodded, and Sara said, "You can't lie to him, Vickie. If you are lying about any of this, one, you will go to jail and, two, there will be no way my husband can protect you."

"I swear to God I will tell him the truth. I will tell him everything I know. I just want to stay alive and help keep my friends alive if I can." Sara nodded as the three women sat in silence waiting for John.

The two story rebuild at the corner of Wynne Avenue and Domino Street in Reseda had been constructed after the nineteen ninety-four Northridge earthquake. The house sat on a beautifully manicured corner lot. Brad and Margo Dell had purchased the home just before the quake and, fortunately, had earthquake insurance, which built them a much better home than the one they originally purchased. Brad was a meticulous landscaper and kept an immaculate home. It was one of the perks of the relationship. She was a practicing up and coming young lawyer with no time to cook and clean, and Brad's life as a teacher left him with summers off and weekends, evenings, and holidays to care for both of their needs.

Brad was standing at the sink rinsing vegetables for dinner when his cell phone rang. He dried his hands and answered it. "Hi baby, it's me. Are you looking forward to tonight?" Brad smiled as he walked back over to the sink and started to cut and chop and said, "Am I? Where to begin…it's been a while. Are you ready for tonight?" "Oh, you know it. I can't wait to feel you inside of me, pumping and grinding…oh I'm creaming myself just thinking about it." Brad had an erection growing in his gray sweat pants, and he said, "Don't start the dirty talk now…I will end up having to hit the couch and beat off before you get here…I have one stuck in the chamber. It's just for you." "Okay, well, I just wanted to call and, stroke, I mean stoke the fire a bit for you. I will have you in my mouth really, really soon. Love you." Brad was rubbing his crotch as he talked and said, "I can't wait for you to take me in your mouth. Love you, too." He hung up the phone and continued fixing dinner.

Mark hung up, and the look on Tim and Jerry's faces was priceless. He laughed and said, "You wanted me to 'stroke' the man and make sure we are on. Well, we're on." Jerry said, "I love you? Really? You love the guy?" Mark didn't say anything. He just undressed and walked into Tim's bathroom to take a shower. He spoke as the water ran over his body. "Yes…in my own way I do love him. I'm sad for Brad. He can't come out, and he will end up dying in a love triangle, or what we have made look like a love triangle between his wife and his boss."

Tim was sitting on the floor with his laptop open, working in the deep web. He was typing away and asking Mark questions until he got what he was looking for. "Got it!" Tim said. "Got what?" asked Mark. "I have the video feed from Brad's security cameras in his house. Now, we can watch the whole thing 'blow by blow.'" Tim and Jerry heard the water shut off, and Mark came walking bare ass into the room. He had a raging hard on, and Jerry said, "Damn, man, you look like your cock is about to explode." "It is. I like getting fucked up the ass. I like sucking cock. I'm not ashamed of it. It's who I am. I'm comfortable with my sexuality. You two morons don't know how good it feels to take it up the ass, so don't judge me. Just throw me my bag, so I can get dressed and try to get this woody down before I do explode all over this room."

Tim grabbed the bag off the bed and said, "Jerry knows what it's like, and he doesn't like it, neither do I. Unless you forgot…the rape started this mess." "You guys are just a bunch of pussies. So, you had a new sexual encounter. Chalk it up to experience and move on, man." Tim got up and walked up to Mark and got in really close to his face then whispered, "When I was killing Rocky, I reminded him what he did to me, how he humiliated me. I don't know what Jerry told Brian, but I told Rocky just how I felt. I'm not a queer. You're a queer. Just remember what Brad helped the others do to you in that school bathroom several months ago. Was that love, man? Is that how that dude loves you? Letting four guys shove bottles and pipes up your ass? That's your idea of fun? Two weeks spent in the hospital telling no one who did that to you? If that was fun, then you don't need to deal with Brad, I will. Your understanding of love is fucked up."

Mark pulled away, his erection gone, and said, "No…what they helped those guys do to me was not love…it was brutal, and it hurt, and I'm lucky to have survived it." Tim pulled away and went back to his sitting position with his laptop. He looked up at Mark who was putting on a black shirt and said, "We are not going to watch you getting ass banged or giving this sicko head. We will tune in at ten for the killings, that's all." Mark nodded as he finished dressing. Tim and Jerry talked about some work they were doing on the deep web while Mark finished getting ready. Jerry asked when Alan was coming by, and Tim told him he didn't know.

Jerry asked if he had heard from Alan, and Tim told him he was online with him as they spoke in a deep web chat room about the killings they were planning. Jerry leaned back and said, "I have a night with Vickie, so I'm going to split. She wants a romantic dinner in exchange for letting me play out my sexual fantasies." Tim shook his head and said, "Man, don't hurt her like you did a while back. She's a messed up kid. You really literally and figuratively fucked her up. And on that note, does she know that she is your half sister?"

Jerry shook his head and said, "I don't see any reason to tell her. She doesn't know that my old man knocked up my mom and her sister and that's how Vickie was born." Tim looked down into his laptop and said, "Your father was a sick fuck…he fucked your mom, raped her sister, who was married to that Delgato guy, and no one ever talked about it. The best thing your old man did for that family was off himself last year." Jerry stood up and said, "I still don't buy the suicide by cop deal…I read the note, and I read the reports, but I still don't think my old man wanted to die."

"Yeah…well…he's dead, and I think you should tell Vickie the truth. Your mom and her mom don't know about you two fucking, do they?" "Nope…and they aren't going to…it's not like we are getting married or having kids, man, shit…we are just having some fun. I will tell her eventually but not while I am able to bust a nut in her daily." Mark was finishing dressing and said, "Well, just remember, dude… she might be on birth control, but that shit's not a hundred percent at stopping babies…me and my sister are living fuckin' proof of that. My mom got pregnant while on the pill twice." Jerry shrugged and said, "Yeah, that was back in the stone ages of birth control. They've come a long way. I'm not worried about it, and besides, if she gets pregnant, she would abort. We've talked about it, and she also has a stockpile of morning after pills that Tim's mom got her. It's all good."

Mark buttoned the front of his shirt and said, "Yeah…it's all good, you incest fuckin' porn freak. And you call me names. You're fucking your damn sister…that's just downright creepy." Jerry walked over to Tim's bed and grabbed his own laptop and logged on, not saying another word.

John pulled into police parking at Northridge Hospital just before six p.m. He and Chris jumped out of the car and ran for Karen's office. John had said nothing to Chris the whole way over, so he had no idea what they were walking into. Karen and Sara were sitting in desk chairs silent when they walked in. Sara walked John over to Vickie's chair and said, "Special Agent John Swenson, this is Ms. Vickie Delgato. She has quite a story to tell you about the events of the past few days at her high school."

John sat down across from her, and Chris followed. John pulled out his tablet and said, "Vickie? May I call you Vickie?" She nodded with tears in her eyes. "This is my partner Agent Mantel. Before I ask you any questions, I am required by law to read you your rights. Okay?" She nodded. He read Vickie her rights, and she acknowledged that she understood them and then spent the next hour explaining as best she could the things that had happened, and the things that she was warned were going to happen as John and Chris listened carefully while recording the interview with their tablets. When she had finished telling them everything, John asked for a moment alone with her.

Chris walked Karen and Sara out of the office, and John waited for the door to close. When it did, he asked, "Your friend, Mark, is going to his coach's house to have sex tonight?" "Yes, sir." "What time?" Vickie looked over at the clock on the wall. It was half past six. "Well, I think he's probably there or on his way there right now. Mark is gay, Agent Swenson. He really thinks that Coach Brad loves him, even though he's married. I have known Mark my whole life, and I don't think he has it in him to hurt anyone. If anything, he will end up telling Coach Dell the plot, and he will end up getting killed himself. Brad has a bad temper, and he's a real asshole."

John nodded and typed Dell's address information into his tablet. He wasn't surprised that Dell had a rap sheet, but he was surprised that he had multiple child sex charges over the past twenty years and was a coach at a major high school. Vickie was watching his face and could see the intensity on his face. She said, "Coach Dell's a bad man, isn't he?" John nodded as a tear rolled down Vickie's cheek. "Can you save Mark, Agent Swenson?" "I will do my best. I am going to have Agent Mantel take you with him into protective custody for the time being."

Vickie shot up out of the chair and said, "No, Agent Swenson, you can't do that. If I disappear now, everyone will know that I ratted them out, and who knows what they will do. I'm having dinner with Jerry Pinskey tonight and then sex. If I stand him up, all hell will break loose. You don't know the type of temper Jerry has. You have to let me go home. I have to keep up appearances." John sat looking at the girl's face and then his tablet. He called for Chris and said, "Listen, you are in charge of protecting Ms. Delgato. She has a date with one of the killers tonight. I want you to make sure she makes her date and then keep an eye on her."

John looked at Vickie and said, "You will go on your date, and when you are finished you will meet Agent Mantel at a location that he directs you to, and you will be in protective custody from there. Are we clear?" Vickie nodded her head slowly as John rose from the chair. Vickie looked up at him in awe and said, "I have never seen someone so big and muscular." John shook his head and said, "Don't flirt with me, kid. It isn't going to help you. You just do what you are told, and I will see about saving your young friend." She nodded and walked over to Chris. John called out to Sara and asked, "Can Chris borrow your car? I have to take care of some business, and he needs to take care of Ms. Delgato." Sara threw Chris her keys and said that she would get a ride home from Karen.

John walked out the office door, and Chris asked Sara, "Where the hell is he going?" Sara and Karen looked at each other, and Sara said, "Hell, if I'm not mistaken." Chris and Vickie just stared at Sara until he took her by the arm and led her out of the building.

The Elliot house was quiet when two of Jim's deputies showed up and knocked on the door. It was just six p.m., and the two deputies stood patiently knocking with no response. Tim heard the knock as Mark was getting ready to leave the house. Tim pulled up the cameras he told his mother he installed for security and saw two sheriffs' deputies standing on his front porch. "Oh, holy fuckin' shit, man." Mark and Jerry were looking at Tim's sheet white face and moved around to see what he was seeing. Jerry saw the cops and said, "That's not a social call, guys. They are here for us…who the fuck blabbed?" They looked at each other and shrugged. "Are there any lights on in the main house?" Jerry asked, and Tim shook his head. "When is your mom due home?" "Any damn minute, man. Shit. Do you think they have a search warrant?"

Jerry looked at the deputies on the front porch and said, "No…if they had a search warrant, they would not be knocking on the door. We have to get the fuck out of here. Is your car parked in the alley?" Tim nodded, and Mark said, "Mine is parked back there, too. I have to get to Brad's. I'm sure we can make a break for it out Tim's window." Jerry looked down at Tim's screen and said, "I'm not worried about getting out of here right now. I'm worried about the plan and who blabbed. Where the fuck is Debbie?" "She had study hall. She will be here later. I know what you're thinking, but there is no way that she said a word. Fuck, man, she killed two chicks."

Tim grabbed a duffle bag and started stuffing it with clothes. Jerry looked at him and asked, "What about our stash of weapons? We can't just leave them here…they might not have a search warrant now, but if this escalates, and they can't find us, they will get one, especially if someone is talking to the cops." Tim shook his head as he turned his laptop now in a split screen showing the GPS coordinates of Alan, Debbie, Jerry and himself. "No way. Everyone that knows about this plot is where they are supposed to be. I haven't told anyone about anything we are doing. What about you, Mark?" He shook his head. "Jerry, you're the mastermind of this operation. Did you tell anyone?" He shook his head. "Well then, all I can figure is the cops got something from the last two crime scenes. But even that doesn't make sense. They would not be knocking on the door.

Tim watched as the two deputies talked into the microphones on their uniforms and then walked away. He paned the camera out to the street and saw the deputies get into two separate cruisers and drive away. Tim said, "Well, whatever they wanted it wasn't that urgent." Jerry looked down at the screen and said, "No. They are off to pick up Alan and Mark. Send Alan a message that he needs to get out of his house." Tim looked down and asked, "Just where the fuck are we all supposed to go, man?" Jerry thought for a second and then said, "Alan's folks have a rental house on Roscoe Boulevard. I know that it's empty. IM him and tell him the situation and see if we can crash there. I've taken Vickie there a couple of times. It's a nice house, fully furnished with a pool and privacy. It's right off Quartz Avenue just on the other side of Reseda Boulevard on the edge of Reseda and Winnetka. We can hide there. Can you move this weaponry?"

Tim nodded and said, "Yeah…but I'm going to need some help, and no one can tell a soul about this or everything will be destroyed." The three boys nodded as Tim opened up the false wall in his closet. He grabbed a couple of boxes and suitcases and started handing weapons to the other two until the closet was clear. They went out the back door and through a doublewide gate into the alley. They put all of the weapons and ammunition into Tim's car and then broke up. Mark drove off to take care of Brad Dell. Tim called Debbie and gave her the location of the new safe house and told her to meet him there. Jerry called Vickie's cell phone but got voicemail. He left her a message that he would be over to pick her up soon and took off for the house with Alan.

CHAPTER EIGHT

"What we are planning would make anyone a little paranoid."

Darkness was settling over the Dell residence when Mark knocked on the front door. It was quiet, and then he heard Brad call to him to come in. He pulled on the screen door and walked into the house to find Brad standing in the kitchen, nude, with a glass of wine in his hand and a smile on his face. There was a lightly lit table setting in the dining room for two. The candlelight glistened off the crystal glasses and water pitcher on the table. The room was homey and warm, and Mark hadn't been in Brad's house in nearly a year. He walked into the kitchen, and Brad grabbed him by the back of the neck and kissed him long and deep. He took Mark's hand and put it on his cock, and Mark slowly moved his hand up and down on Brad's shaft as he started to strip off his clothing. It was easy enough to do; Mark was wearing only a pair of shorts without underwear and a black button up shirt.

The buttons were popping off the shirt as Brad ripped it from his body. Before Mark knew what hit him, he was bent over a dining room chair with Brad grunting and sweating. "Oh, God, I've missed you, Mark…Jesus. When's the last time we fucked?" Mark was trying to get his breath to answer when he felt Brad's cock enlarge and start throbbing deep inside of him. He could feel the semen rushing into his ass, and it took Mark's breath away, and he slumped down as Brad lay across his bare back. There were a few moments of silence, then Brad pulled out and pushed Mark to his knees to finish cleaning up his cock. When the 'sucking and fucking' were over, he said, "Damn, you're a good kid…I wish I could be out of the closet and have you here with me all the time."

Mark was wiping the sides of his mouth as he stood up and said, "But it will never be that way, will it honey?" Brad walked back into the kitchen and poured two glasses of wine and handed one to Mark and said, "You never know. I'm tired of living this lie. I'm going to tell Margo that I'm gay, and that I want a divorce." That rocked Mark back on his heels, and he sat down on a barstool near the kitchen island gently as he could feel Brad's semen trying to escape and said, "So you want to leave Margo for me?" Brad nodded, taking a sip of his wine.

"I do, and I will, but there is something that I want you to do for me." Mark took a sip of the wine and then felt the semen starting to seep out of his rectum. "Just give me a second. I need to use the bathroom. You came hard, and your cum is making a break for it." He ran to the bathroom holding his ass cheeks together while Brad worked on the meal. When he came back he said, "Wow…it has been a while. The toilet was nothing but a sea of blood after I shit out your cum." "Are you in pain? Did I hurt you?" Mark shook his head, taking a sip of the wine and said, "No…it doesn't hurt at all. I figure two months without anal, and after what happened to me in the school bathroom, it will take time to get back in shape. Now, what is it that you want from me?"

Brad put some cheese and fruit on a plate with some crackers and grabbed Mark by the shoulder and said, "Come with me. Let's have a snack and talk in the bedroom." There was candlelight and soft music playing in the master suite, and Mark could see the outline of the shotgun next to the bedroom door, leaning against Brad's dresser. Brad fed Mark a few grapes and said, "I want you to kill my wife." Mark chewed slowly and asked, "Why don't you do it?" "You know and I know that I will be the prime suspect. But if you happen to knock her on the head and put her body in the trunk of your car, I'm sure you could get with some of your buddies and take care of her."

Mark stopped eating and looked at him and asked, "What do you mean by, 'me and my buddies?'" Brad laughed and said, "I saw Jerry and Brian at the bleachers the other night. I know what Jerry did to Brian. I also know that Tim killed Rocky." Mark was silent for several minutes, and Brad asked, "Cat got your tongue?" Mark shook his head and said, "I really don't know what you're talking about." Brad stood up, his husky muscular six foot frame nude in the candlelight. He grabbed a whip out of the closet and then took Mark by the hand and put him in a leather restraint on his knees and said, "Well, I will just have to fuck and beat the memory out of you." He grabbed a bottle of lube and started to slather it on as Mark pleaded with him not to hurt him.

The black Silverado pulled into a back alley behind the Dell home. It was half past nine. The Eagle stepped out of the truck in his full body armor with a small satchel of zip ties and duct tape. He had a tranquilizer gun on his hip, and he moved to the back gate of the house and entered in silence. The Eagle pressed a button on the side of his mask, and the integrated night vision that he had been working on to make his movements more fluid lit up. He could see a small Jacuzzi, and he could also hear murmurs and whimpers coming from a pair of sliding doors on the far end of the house. He moved toward the sound and saw Mark Rubio on his knees with a larger man behind him, pounding away. The Eagle moved to the doors, and they were open.

Mark was unable to speak. He was just grunting and trying to catch his breath. Brad was pounding away on him and telling him he knew what his friends had done. Brad raised his arm to strike Mark on his back when he felt a sharp pain in the side of his neck. It was only momentary, and he slipped into unconsciousness and out of Mark. Mark looked over to see Brad on the floor, and he started to call to him while resisting and trying to release himself from the restraints when a large, dark figure stepped into the bedroom. Mark looked up to see the pale green eyes of the Eagle's mask looking down at him. Mark opened his mouth to scream, but the Eagle put his fingers to his lips and said, "You are already in a lot of trouble, Mr. Rubio. Don't heap any more onto it." The Eagle shot him with a tranquilizer dart then took both men to his truck, leaving no calling card and the house untouched.

Margo Dell walked through the front door at nine thirty and was greeted by candlelight and the smell of garlic chicken. She walked through the formal living room and into the dining room to see a place setting for two and candles burning on the table. She called out to Brad, but the only thing that greeted her call was silence. She walked back to the master bedroom, but it was empty. She searched the house but found no sign of her husband other than a spilled bottle of lube, a leather whip, some clothing, and a small black bag on the bedroom floor.

Chris dropped Vickie off two doors from her house and watched her head up the walk and go in. He sat and waited for her date to arrive, all the while asking himself, "Where did John go? Why isn't he in on this surveillance?"

Jerry pulled off Tunney Avenue in Reseda into an alley that separated the lower income blue-collar homes in the more depressed area of the city. He parked outside of Vickie's house and looked around for any sign of people or vehicles. There was no one else around, and he pushed the broken wood gate on Vickie's house open and knocked on the back door. At first he thought she wasn't there. He pulled out his phone to call her when the porch light came on, and the door cracked open. Vickie was still dressed in the same clothes from school, and Jerry said, "That's what you're wearing for dinner in a fancy restaurant?" She shook her head and opened the door wide and said, "Come in. I just got home. I haven't had the chance to change." He followed her to her bedroom and watched as she undressed and walked into the single bathroom and started the shower. Jerry was impatient with her and said, "Jesus, Vickie, if I knew you were going to have to do a full fuckin' presentation, I would have brought a damn video game to play." She frowned and stepped into the shower and talked as the water ran over her body.

"So, what's going on? I saw I missed a call from you, but I didn't listen to your message." Jerry sat down on the toilet across from the shower and said, "We have had to make some new accommodations for the guys as well as Deb and you. The sheriff's department showed up at Tim's, and I'm pretty certain that they are heading for each of our houses." Vickie was washing her hair and asked, "You guys didn't answer the door?" "No." "If you didn't, then how the hell do you know they were there about you or Tim or any of the guys? Maybe they were there for something else."

Jerry looked through the clear curtain where Vickie was washing her breasts and body and had slowly moved down to her legs. "What the fuck, Vickie? Do you think that we're paranoid?" "A little bit, yeah!" Jerry just watched her turn her back to him and bend over to shave her legs. He commented on her ass and legs. She laughed and thanked him before shutting off the water and drying off. Jerry was distracted, and she could tell.

"So, what do you think? Do you think that maybe you guys are getting paranoid?" Jerry looked over as she was drying her hair. He waited until she shut off the dryer, so he didn't have to compete with the noise. "What we are planning would make anyone a little paranoid.

I would rather be paranoid than get my ass caught before we can carry out the killings." Vickie was pulling on a slinky red dress. She had no bra and no panties, and the low cut dress had a small amount of elastic to hold her ample cleavage. She spoke as she put lotion on her legs, "You killed Brian, Jerry. Tim killed Rocky, and Deb killed Greta and Beth. You sent Mark on a suicide mission to kill Brad Dell. You know as well as I do that he won't be able to do it, and he is most likely either giving him head or getting fucked right now and loving it. Your plan is going to fall apart. You would be better off just dropping out of sight."

Jerry sat back on the toilet seat and said, "You sure know a lot, Vickie. I don't recall giving you all those details. Who have you been talking to, or more importantly, who has been talking to you?" Vickie put on some makeup and was brushing her hair. "Debbie told me everything that she knows. We're best friends. She told me about what you guys are planning, and now that Brian is dead…and I'm not sad about that…I know that you killed him. Deb told me about the stockpile of weapons that Tim has at the house, and she warned me to stay away from homecoming. Come on, Jerry. I don't need a full page ad in the *Times* to know what you're planning. What Tim, Alan, and Mark are putting together with you. You want revenge. You want to take out your aggression for the beatings, the bullying, and the bad shit that you have gone through at the hands of so many for so many years." She paused and looked at Jerry's downturned face and continued, "You know damn well you feel bad about what you did to Brian, and I know Timmy way too well. He may not show it on the outside, but inside what he did to Rocky is tearing him apart. As for Mark…I'm sorry, but he is not going to do anything other than probably confess to Coach Dell that he planned to kill him tonight because Dell allowed Brian and the boys to rape and torture him a few months ago. It's falling apart, Jerry. The plan is falling apart."

Jerry jumped off the toilet seat and grabbed Vickie by the throat. He pulled her close to his face as he choked her. "What the fuck are you doing, you little bitch? Who the fuck have you talked to outside of Debbie and me?" Vickie was choking and gasping for air as his grip got tighter around her neck. Her eyes were bulging, and she was trying to say, "No one…no one…I swear…no one."

Chris was sitting in the car watching Vickie's home. He saw the lights come on at the back, and he was looking at the gray frosted glass of the lighted bathroom window and the light coming through it. He looked down at his watch, and it had been nearly forty-five minutes, so he opened the car door and headed toward the house, listening for any sound. He heard clipped and hushed conversation and then the sound of glass breaking. He ran for the front door with his weapon drawn.

Jerry had lifted Vickie off the floor with both hands wrapped around her throat. She was struggling to breathe and fight him. She swung her right arm widely and struck the bathroom mirror, breaking it and sending shards of glass into the sink. Jerry held her tight in his grip and said, "You little bitch…you're the one who got the cops to the house. You're the one who's talking out there, you fuckin' cunt." Jerry threw Vickie down onto the bathroom floor, and she gasped for air as he pulled a knife from his waistband and pointed it at her. "You won't talk to anyone else, you little cunt. I'll make sure of that." He started for her as she pushed her back against the bathroom wall and attempted to scream.

Jerry stopped when he heard the sound of breaking glass and a male voice call out, "FBI!" He looked down at Vickie then ran out of the bathroom, jumping through her front bedroom window and running around the corner to the alley and took off in his car. Chris was calling out to her as he cleared room by room with his weapon. He heard her strained voice coming from the bathroom and found her on the floor, her dress hiked up to her throat, her hands at her sides, and her neck purple and swollen. Chris felt for her pulse as she stared off into space, her breathing heavily labored. He called 911 and an ambulance was on its way. He picked her up and laid her on her bed. She looked into his eyes and said in a raspy voice, "I told you he would get to me. He's killed me."

Chris stroked her hair and said, "You're going to be fine, Vickie. You're going to be just fine. Who did this?" "Jerry. Jerry Pinskey. He's losing it. He's going to do worse." Vickie was blacking out as the ambulance sirens were approaching the house. Chris looked at her slowly dilating eyes and said, "Stay with me, Vickie…hold on just a few more seconds." He heard the EMTs calling out and yelled out his location. They got in the room and began working on her as he walked out into the front room, pacing, waiting, needing to know that the young girl he was responsible for was going to be okay. There was a flurry of action all around him, yet he stood silent, staring as the paramedics rolled Vickie out with a ventilator bag on her throat. They rushed passed him, and he called out, "What hospital?" "Northridge."

LAPD had arrived on scene, and Chris gave instructions and then called for his own FBI team to get into the house and gather evidence. He called John's cell phone but got voicemail. He left a message explaining what happened, and that he was on his way to Northridge Hospital to make sure Vickie was going to be all right. He jumped into his car and while driving at breakneck speed called Jim and asked him to meet him at the hospital.

CHAPTER NINE

"Do innocent people have to die?"
"I guess so...I'm innocent, and
according to you, I'm dying."

"I'm cold," Mark said to an empty but well-lit room. He was nude and had been left the way the Eagle found him along with Brad, who was asleep on a gurney next to him, nude as well. Mark could see his breath, and he called out, but there was no response. "Jesus, I'll die of exposure at this rate." He tried to move but was unable to, although he wasn't restrained. He called out again, and a large hulking figure dressed in white with a surgeon's mask walked up to the table and towered over him.

"Who are you?" "That's not important at this moment, Mr. Rubio. Do you want to tell me of the plans being hatched by you and your friends?" Mark looked away and over to Brad on the gurney next to him. "Why isn't Brad awake?" "Because I don't want him awake yet, Mark. Answer my question." "Brad and I have been lovers for nearly four years. His wife doesn't know he's gay. He told me before you came to his house that he was divorcing her and coming out of the closet to be with me."

“What else did he tell you?” There was a pause in Mark’s breathing, and the Eagle looked down to see him staring wide-eyed at Brad. The Eagle struck him on the chest, and he started to breathe again. He turned his head to see the Eagle staring back at him and asked, “Who are you?” “The person who is going to stop you and your friends.”

Mark looked away again and said, “Not going to happen. I was supposed to kill Brad tonight, but I knew I couldn’t do it. He told me he knew of our plan, too, but I doubt that he could really have any idea of what is going on, or that you could stop it.” The Eagle pulled out a tablet and pressed a button on the screen, and the room’s cameras came to life. Mark could see himself on several video monitors in the room. He looked back at the Eagle and asked, “When are you going to kill me?” The Eagle rapped on the side of the gurney and said, “For your sake, your death is going to take care of itself.”

“I don’t understand,” Mark said. “I know about your injuries from the rape and beating that you received a few months ago. I have looked over your medical history. Tonight was the first time you’ve had anal sex since the incident, wasn’t it?” Mark nodded slowly. His head was getting foggy. “Yea…but…um…I was having a great time. I’m feeling a little tired and weak.” The Eagle stood up and started an IV and gave him an injection of adrenalin. His eyes fluttered, and he became more animated.

“Wow! What the fuck did you give me?” “Adrenaline. It will buy us a little more time as you bleed out.” “Bleed out?” The Eagle nodded. “Your injuries were fixed after the attack, but, unfortunately, your rectum still needed at least a year of healing and probably more surgery before you could engage in anal sex. Your lover over there,” the Eagle pointed to Dell, “is the one who killed you. When he put his penis in you, he ripped out that delicately healing tissue, and you’re now bleeding to death. So… since you’re going to be dead in a few minutes, do you want to tell me about the plot, or are you going to take it to the grave with you?”

Mark’s face turned to one of sheer panic. He cried out, “You’re lying to me; you’re lying about all of this. You want to scare me into telling you our plans.” “I’m telling you the truth, and with each second that you lie there yelling and screaming, you get that much closer to death and that much farther from helping me stop those involved in this plot. Do innocent people have to die?" Mark laughed and said, "I guess so…I'm innocent, and according to you, I'm dying." The Eagle leaned in close and said, "Tell me about the plan and who's involved."

As Mark began to lose consciousness, the Eagle gave him another shot of adrenalin, and he woke a little but not near as much as he had a few minutes before. "It's too late, man…if you found me, then you know who the others are. I don't know for sure when they plan to attack. There is still unfinished personal business between some of the attackers and their bullies. What do you care? Who the hell are you?" Mark was starting to slip away, and the Eagle said, "I'm the Iron Eagle." As Mark's pupils began dilating, his last words were, "Of all the people to be after us, it has to be you…you will kill them all. It's just a matter of if you catch them before, during, or after. Brad claimed he knew of the plot. Ask…him."

After Mark died, the Eagle closed his eyes and turned his attention to Dell. He set an IV line on the sleeping man and prepared to wake him.

Jim got to Northridge Hospital and met up with Chris in the ER. Chris was frazzled, and Jim asked, "So, what the fuck, Chris…what's going on?" Chris sat down in one of the waiting room chairs and said, "I fucked up, Jim. I really fucked up. Jerry Pinskey got to her and nearly strangled her to death. Sara and Karen are working on her now." Jim sat down next to him and said, "Listen, kid…you're not going to save them all, and you're not always going to make the right call. You figured the guy would come to the front door, right?" Chris nodded. "Well, you fucked up. Did you know the house backed up to an alley?" Chris shook his head. "The first rule of police work, man, know your fuckin' stakeout. You need to know entrance and exit points when you're protecting a witness. Didn't they teach you that at Quantico?" Chris nodded, and Jim took a cigarette out of his top left pocket and put it in his mouth.

"Follow me. I need a smoke." As he stood up, Chris asked, "What about the girl?" "What about her? She's in the hands of two great doctors. There's nothing you can do for her now. It's up to them. Take a walk with me. I need a smoke, and you need to clear your damn head."

Chris followed Jim outside to a small bench with a concrete ashtray and a sign that said, 'smoking area.' Jim pulled out his Zippo, lit the smoke, and took a couple of deep hits off it. "So, we know that this Jerry Pinskey kid is bad news." "Yeah…I didn't know how bad." Jim laughed, "He's a bad guy, Chris. Trust me. Anyone who would attempt to kill a friend is usually a bad guy. I would venture a guess that he's the ring leader in this mess." Jim looked around and asked, "Where the fuck is Swenson?" "I don't know. We interrogated the girl right here, and he told me to take her home and wait for Pinskey, that he had something to do."

Jim took another hit off his cigarette and asked, "What did she tell you two?" "That one of her friends, Mark Rubio, was going to try to kill a teacher tonight. She gave us the details and some other information, and John told me to take her home and he left." Jim nodded, blowing smoke out his nose and mouth. It rose up the right side of his face and made his eye water. "Well…if John's on the move, we will most likely get more information on this situation soon." Chris looked at him and asked, "What the hell does that mean? 'If John's on the move?'" Jim laughed and said, "You have a lot to learn about police work, kid, a whole helluva lot."

Chris started to say something when he saw Sara come out the ER doors into the lobby. He stood up, and Jim followed. Chris didn't like the look on Sara's face. "How is she?" "Her assailant crushed her throat and airway. We were able to perform a tracheotomy, which has restored her ability to breathe, but she's in a coma. She's in extremely serious condition. We need to notify her next of kin. She was without oxygen for over four minutes, so she might have serious brain damage. We won't know for a day or so."

Jim looked at Sara and asked, "Have you done an EEG?" "Yes…she has brain activity; she's not brain dead." Sara looked at Chris and said, "That's a good thing, Chris. It gives me more hope that she will pull through. Where's

John?" "Beats the fuck out of us," Jim said, "Chris says that John got some information out of the girl before the Pinskey kid tried to kill her, and he is on the move." Sara nodded, and Chris asked again, "What the hell would John be on the move on? You two know more about John than you're telling me." Sara laughed and started back into the ER. She said with her back to Chris, "You're kinda slow, Chris, but I'm sure you'll catch up…eventually." Chris looked at Jim who shrugged his shoulders and said, "She's not fuckin' wrong. Come on. We need to get to this girl's house and the crime scene and see what… if anything…they have learned."

Jerry made his way to the house on Quartz where Tim and Alan were already working. He walked in out of breath and Tim asked, "What the fuck, man? You look like you've seen a ghost." Jerry sat down at the dining room table where the boys were typing away on their laptops. He said, "I think I killed Vickie." They both looked up, and Tim asked, "You think you did what?" "She's the mole. She's the one who's been talking to the cops. I was at her house, and I confronted her on it. I lost it, man. I just fuckin' lost it and started choking her out when all of a sudden there was a fuckin' FBI agent busting through the front door. I barely got away. I think I killed her. There's no way she can talk. I'm sure of it."

The boys sat silent with shocked looks on their faces. Tim was about to say something when he heard Debbie clear her throat, "You killed my best friend? You killed my best damn friend. OMG! Why?" Jerry looked over at Debbie and said, "Because you have been talking WAY TOO MUCH. You told her too much, and she was in contact with the cops. The sheriffs on Tim's front stoop…that was no joke. They were looking for us…all of us."

Debbie sat down next to Tim and asked Jerry, "Did she tell you that?" "She didn't have to. I know it. I called one of my neighbors, and he told me that the sheriff was at my house looking for me and wanted to talk to me. He told me that the deputies left a card with him and asked him to call when I came home. They are most likely going from house to house, Deb, and it's your damn fault." She sat up straight and said, "Vickie has no idea the depth of this plot, Jerry. She knew that you killed Brian and about Tim and me and what happened with Rocky as well as Greta and Beth."

"Did she know about Mark and what he's doing as we speak?" Debbie fell silent. Jerry yelled, "DID SHE KNOW ABOUT MARK AND WHAT HE'S DOING, YOU LITTLE BITCH?" Debbie was looking down at the tabletop. He threw a glass across the room, and it smashed into the wall. "You have no idea what you have done, do you Deb? You have compromised our whole fuckin' mission. Years of planning, plotting, working to get these fuckers where we want them, and you spout off, and your friend tells the cops. I don't need her to tell me she did it…for fuck's sake, the goddamn sheriff and FBI are looking for us. If they get their hands on any of us, we are as good as dead. Do you understand what you've done?" Jerry's voice was hoarse and strained as he asked her the question.

Tears started running down her face, and Tim looked at her and asked, "Did you really do that, Debbie? Did you tell Vickie the whole plot?" "She was my best friend. We tell each other everything. I told her some stuff, but I did not tell her about the whole plot." "What else did you tell her?" There was silence, and Alan said, "I have a lead in the chat room in underground five who says that word on the street is the cops are looking for us." Alan turned his laptop screen, so Tim could read the messages. "What else did you tell Vickie?" There was a moment of silence between all of them, and she said in a soft voice, "I told her to stay away from school on homecoming." Jerry shot to his feet and reached out for her, but Alan and Tim got between them.

"YOU TOLD HER?" Tim and Alan were restraining him as he fought to get to Debbie. "So what now, Jerry? I fucked up. I made a mistake. I trusted my best friend…are you going to kill me now? Or maybe Tim or Alan? They know everything about the plot. Keep killing us and you will be alone in this mess." Jerry shook free and walked into the living room and paced, talking to himself as he walked. He looked at them and asked, "Have you heard from Mark?" They shook their heads. "What about you, princess talks a lot? Have you heard from him?" She shook her head. "I don't think this is a safe location," Alan said, looking at his laptop and a message that had popped up on his screen. The message was cryptic but pointed. *'They know where you are...you don't have much time to get out and find a new crib.'*

Tim just shook his head and said, "Thanks, Debbie. You turned our lives into a nightmare instead of us doing that to those who hurt us." Jerry looked at the three of them and said, "I know of another house. It belonged to my aunt and is vacant in Northridge. We can stay there, and there is no way that anyone on the planet will find us." Tim asked, "What about your friend? The cops and now the feds are going to lean on him?" "I'm fine. No one knows." Jerry looked over at Alan and asked, "What do your folks know about this plot?" "Nothing...not a damn thing. I have a desktop computer at home, but the cops and feds can sweep that hard drive. They won't find anything. I have been doing everything on TOR in the deep web."

"What about your Internet activity on social media?" Alan laughed. "I post general shit. All they will find are hate messages from people from school. Everyone hates me. Shit, I must have two dozen messages that are telling me to kill myself because I'm a loser." Jerry asked Tim the same questions. "I have no digital footprint that would point here in the standard web. I have the same hate messages that Alan talks about, saying the same things, that I should off myself. My hard drive is clean. Everything I do is on TOR and is on this laptop and my tablet...and both are with me. My mother knows nothing, but my father is a different story.

"He and I video chat at least once a week. I do it on my laptop, and it is encrypted by me and the government. My old man knows what I'm going through. He's the one who has been smuggling in the weapons and the ammunition we have for the plot. I think he thinks it's a game; at least he talks like we are playing a role play war game. He's been shipping me all the weapons we have, claiming he is stocking in case the worst happens. He has no idea I intend to use them on the school and my enemies." Jerry looked at Debbie and asked, "What about you?"

"Only Vickie…I'm the same as the rest of you. My social status is up to date, and I have tons of messages about how much of a loser I am and how I should kill myself, too. I don't know a damn thing about TOR nor have I ever mentioned it, not even to Vickie. My folks don't even know where I am, nor do they care. I live with Tim for the most part, so they are no threat." Tim looked at Jerry and asked, "What about you, Jerry? Are you clean? You are the king of this plot. Is there anything on your computers that could lead the cops to us?"

Jerry looked at the three faces staring at him and said, "My laptop has all of my TOR deep web information. It's password protected and encrypted, but it's also at my house. I haven't been home since killing Brian. If the cops are on to us and they serve a search warrant, they could get my laptop." "Great…you're in charge, and your shit is sitting at home just waiting for someone to take it." Jerry said, "It doesn't matter. We haven't mentioned anything in our manifesto about where we're going to strike. We'll still get a high kill rate at homecoming even though it's been moved off-campus.

"Sunday night at the Northridge Mall in one of the empty Anchor department stores. Everyone who is anyone in school will be there, plus all of the teachers and administrators. We can get a great kill rate, and we also can escape easily after we have hit them with everything we have." Alan and Tim sat back down, as did Debbie, and started typing. Jerry was calmer and said, "You did wrong, Deb. You put the whole plot in jeopardy not to mention our lives." She nodded. He continued, "Let's hack the database at the mall. We can break in tomorrow night and start setting up bombs and trip mines at the emergency exits. When the shooting starts, they will all run. There will be hundreds of the fuckers and for every one who makes it to an exit, they will just blow more and more of the group to hell." Tim and Alan nodded as they typed. Debbie sat silent as Jerry paced, talking to himself and them about the new plan to open up a rampage on those who had done them wrong.

Brad Dell awoke to the smell of burning flesh and a pain in the middle of his chest. He was still groggy and not sure what was happening until he realized the flesh that was burning was his own, and that a large man dressed in white was pressing a steel rod hard into the middle of his chest. Brad felt the pain of the branding iron and tried to scream but could not get his breath. He moved his head from side to side as his assailant continued. When the rod was taken away, the smell of flesh and the agony of the burns took hold, and he started screaming. The Eagle put the branding iron down and gave Brad an injection of a pain killer. Brad's pain level began dropping, and he became happier. He looked at the masked man and asked, "Why are you doing this to me?"

The Eagle pointed to Mark. "Who are you?" "I'm the Iron Eagle, and the kid is dead. He died as a result of your sex acts on him this evening and injuries he sustained as a result of your actions and the actions of Coach Trent Hameln. Do you remember what you two allowed to happen to this kid who says he was your lover?" Brad looked over at Mark's still corpse, and his eyes filled with tears. "He's dead?" "Yes, Mr. Dell, he's dead and not as a result of anything that I did to him. He's dead because of your actions and inactions. He did tell me before he died that you claim to know of a plot that he and his friends are involved in. Is that true?" Dell winced against the restraints the Eagle had running across the upper part of his chest. They pressed down on the burnt flesh where the Iron Eagle had branded him.

"I don't know, really. I was talking out of my ass. I'm a damn teacher, and I hear all kinds of shit. There is always some campus conspiracy going on." The Eagle sat down next to Brad and asked, "And what conspiracy theory or story did you hear about that included your lover over there?" "Oh, Jesus, Mark's dead. Oh my God!" The Eagle slapped Brad on the side of the face and said, "Yes, the kid is dead; you can't bring him back. He is dead because of your actions, and I have plans for you, so if you want to try to mitigate the agony I will inflict on you, tell me what you have heard, fact or fiction. I will sort it out."

Brad started to cry, and the Eagle struck him hard across the brand and even the pain medication could not control the agony of the third degree burn. He let out a yelp and said, "There's a story that some of the nerdy kids are planning an attack on the school. I reported it to the principal and law enforcement as I am required, but the story has been circulating throughout the school for over a year. It was investigated, and there was no credibility to it." "Then why bring it up with the kid?" "I was trying to scare him…he liked bondage and scare tactics, but the kid was as gentle as a kitten. He couldn't hurt a fly." "You loved him, but you allowed him to be beaten and raped by four students?" Brad smacked his head back on the gurney with tears running down his face. He said, "It was a situation that just got out of control. It wasn't supposed to go that way."

"Then why didn't you stop it?" "They would know if I stopped it." "That you're gay?" Brad nodded, weeping. The Eagle looked on and said, "This kid is not the first for you, is it Mr. Dell? You have raped several young boys." "I never raped anyone; it was consensual sex with boys who were grappling with their sexuality. I just helped them come out." The Eagle let out a muted laugh and said, "Yet you remained in the closet?" "I never meant for any of this to happen. I loved Mark. I truly did. I was going to tell my wife tonight that I was leaving her. I was going to come out."

The Eagle pulled over a steel table of instruments covered with a white cloth. Brad looked at the table and then the Eagle and said, "The story is that Mark and some friends…" "Names, please," said the Eagle as he worked with some apparatus next to the gurney. "Um…Jerry Pinskey, Tim Elliott, um…Alan Marks and Mark. They supposedly are working through TOR in the deep web to set up an attack on the school and their classmates who have injured them." "Injured them? You mean beating them up? Bullying them?" The Eagle had pulled a long cord across Brad's body. He pressed down on a foot pedal on the floor, and Brad heard the whir of a dentist's drill.

He started to speak more quickly and with a great deal of fear in his voice. “Um…they were supposedly going to attack the school. Some of the kids that were bullying them didn’t just beat them up…I mean, that was part of it…but a few of the guys were in scouts with the boys, and there was an incident a couple of years ago at a sleep over.” The Eagle pulled the white cloth off the small steel tray to reveal all kinds of steel instruments, sharp pointed steel probes, pliers, and curved steel blades, all in Brad’s line of sight. Brad heaved a deep breath as he saw them. The Eagle never looked up, only asked, “What happened, who were the boys that were hurt, and who hurt them?”

“Um….please, please. I will tell you everything I know. Please don’t use those things on me. I’m terrified of the dentist.” “What happened, Mr. Dell?” “The boys I mentioned were raped in their tent by some bullies…umm…Brian Donaldson, who’s now dead, Rocky Marick, who has also been murdered, along with two other boys, Johnny Belk and Billy Stone.” “Were you and Mr. Hameln there?” “I was not there, but Trent Hameln was. He’s a scout leader. He told me about it a few months after the fact. The boys all stayed silent about what was done to them.”

The Eagle pointed the drill at Brad and said, “Yeah…until now. So the killings are revenge for what these guys did to them?” “I don’t know. I guess so. I don’t know anything else, other than these boys that Mark was friends with worked in the deep web through some site called TOR, and I think that it’s all fiction.” The Eagle laid the drill and its hose across Brad’s abdomen and said, “TOR is not fiction… the deep web is not fiction. TOR is an Internet web browser that was developed originally by the U.S. Navy for encrypted communication over the Internet. The government abandoned the project, but the TOR web browser continued on into the world of the Internet that is known as ‘the onion.’ TOR allows users to work in anonymity without the regular tracers that come with working on the standard Internet. The NSA, FBI, CIA, and local law enforcement use the site to both try to detect criminal activity and to pass secure data between agencies. TOR is very real and, if used inappropriately by these ‘nerds’ as you call them, could give them a forum to gain power, support, and even the equipment and weapons they need to carry out their attacks.

"In your case, ignorance is bliss, but the reality of what could be hatched by these students if they are computer literate and can write code could be terrifying. Thank you for the information. I can work with this and hopefully foil their plot." The Eagle pulled a steel dental cage off the table and pushed Brad's head back as he placed it over his jaw and teeth. Brad fought him at first, but the Eagle subdued him with two quick blows to the head, and by the time Brad got his bearings, his mouth was wired open. He was unable to speak, and the Eagle was pressing his elbow into the brand on his chest as he began to drill out tooth after tooth. His screams of agony fell on deaf ears. Smoke rose in the air, and the smell of burning tooth enamel and decay filled the operating room.

When the Eagle finished drilling and spraying ice water into Brad's mouth, blood, spit, and tooth fragments were striking Brad in the face. Some got into his left eye, and he screamed louder and louder as he tried to blink them out. But with each blink, he tore through the sclera of his eye, and soon he felt a warm liquid flowing down his face as the vision in the eye vanished.

The Eagle stepped back and looked at Brad's torn eyeball and said, "This is a first for me. You blinked your own dental work into your eye, tearing the sclera and opening up a hole and releasing the vitreous humor. You're blind now." The Eagle then pulled a long steel twisted instrument from the table and made sure Brad could see it with his remaining eye. "This looks kind of like a cork screw, and you have no need for that eye anymore." The Eagle drove the instrument into the eyeball until he met resistance near the back of the eye socket. He twisted as Brad screamed, and with a hard straight jerk pulled his eyeball out of its socket and laid it on his chest. The optic nerve was the only thing connecting the eyeball to his skull, and the Eagle quickly cut it with a pair of scissors, which sent Brad's body into convulsions as the Eagle lifted the removed eye up so he could see it. "I know that has to hurt like hell. The eyeball itself has no nerves, but the optic nerve does. Well, back to work. You have more to endure, but don't you worry. You are going to make a very, very strong impression on all of those young kids."

It was just after eleven p.m. when Brad Dell drew his last labored and agonizing breath. The Eagle cleaned up the corpse and prepared it for transport. When he was finished, he walked out of the operating room, removed his white coveralls, and walked out into the foyer of his lair. He pulled out his cell phone and waited as his placed call rang.

"WHAT?" "I have some good information on the plot." Jim was sitting in his car outside Vickie's home. "Yeah…well…it came a little too late for Vickie Delgato." John looked out through the blackness of the windows of his lair overlooking the sea and asked as the surf crashed on the rocks below, "What happened?" "Your protégé fucked up. He let the girl go in alone. The Pinskey kid came in the back way through the alley behind her home and choked her out." "Is she dead?" "Yeah. I got the call ten minutes ago from Sara. The girl went into cardiac arrest. Sara said that she and Karen tried but couldn't save her." "And Chris?" "He's fucked up, man. What do you think? He blames himself." "He should…it's his fault that she's dead!" There was a moment of silence, and Jim asked, "Is the Eagle finished?" "He has to drop off a victim to send a message." "Where?" "Brad Dell's home." "I'm going to go out on a short goddamn limb here and say that Mr. Dell is not currently alive."

"Meet me at the Dell home at midnight." Jim sighed. "The Eagle will have a bit of a problem setting up a scene at his home. The fucker's got a wife, man, and I would take a leap that she's home and in bed." "Then you need to find a way to get her out of there." "Oh no…I'm not going to be an accessory to yet another Eagle killing. You want her out, you get her out." "Fine…I'll just shoot her." The line went dead, and Jim yelled, "No, no, no, you mother fucker!"

CHAPTER TEN

"Hell is about to come to dinner."

It was half past eleven, and all was quiet on Osborn Street in Northridge. Jerry had given Tim and Alan the address of the home, and they arrived with Debbie at the dark house tucked back in its own little corner of a dead end street. Jerry pulled up and pulled into the driveway, and in a matter of seconds the garage door was opened, and Tim, Alan, and Debbie were pulling out ammunition and weapons and stowing them in the garage. Jerry told them to park the cars inside and to meet him at the rear of the house when they were done.

The back door was open with a single light on when the three walked in. Jerry told them to close the door. He was sitting at a table in the kitchen. Tim looked around at the house and asked, "What the fuck is this place? Why are you so goddamn sure we won't be found here?" Jerry was looking out the back window as he answered, "This was my aunt's home and was left to me after her passing. This house has a great deal of history behind it, a bloody and insane history." Alan said, "I didn't know you had an aunt who died." Jerry smiled weakly and said, "No one knows about Aunt Charlotte. She was actually my mother's first cousin, but she and I formed a bond through her life. She was killed several months ago in the Topanga mountains."

Debbie got a shocked look on her face and asked, "Are you talking about Charlotte Watson? The psycho baby killer and part of the Richards family?" Jerry nodded. Debbie said, "And this is her childhood home?" He nodded again, and Tim and Alan both asked, "What's the big deal? Jerry inherited a home." Debbie looked at Jerry and then at the other two and said, "No…this is no ordinary home, and his aunt was no ordinary woman. She was a brutal murderer who butchered her whole family in this house some four or five decades ago because Bruno Richards told her to do it, from what I understand."

Tim had a confused look on his face and asked, "Who the hell is Bruno Richards?" "A beautiful mind that was snuffed out before his dreams and prophecies could be realized," Jerry said. Debbie explained the history behind the Richards Family and what she knew of Charlotte Watson. She walked the guys through the house and showed them the blood spattered walls, mattresses, and blood-stained floors, while telling them the story as she knew it from reading several books. When they had finished, Debbie walked the guys back into the kitchen where Jerry was still staring off into space. Tim looked at him and asked, "Dude…Jerry…" Tim snapped his fingers a couple of times, and Jerry looked over at him.

"Are you okay? Did you do some drugs or something?" "I'm fine…this is only the second time I have been in this house and the first time since Charlotte was killed." "Jesus, man, you look lovesick," Alan said. "I am…I had my first sexual experience in this house with her. I don't think she planned for it to happen. I know I didn't, but it did, and it was beautiful." Alan and Tim looked at Debbie who was white-faced. Debbie asked, "Are you going to be okay here? You're starting to freak me and the guys out." He nodded and said, "Get on TOR and see what you can learn about us in the chat rooms. We have a lot to do and a short time to get it done. We need the security codes to get into the mall, so we can start setting our traps."

Tim and Alan opened their equipment and started working in the deep web. Alan came back and said, “So far, there are no wants or warrants for us. You need to get your head together and get to your house and get your computer and whatever other equipment you have.” Jerry nodded and asked Debbie to come with him. She looked at Tim with hesitation and fear in her eyes. Tim said, “No, she won’t. I will go with you. I don’t trust you around her right now, and we don’t need you killing another person tonight.” Tim grabbed his keys and Jerry’s arm and pulled him up out of the chair, and the two walked out to the garage and Tim’s car.

Jim pulled up in front of the Dell home just before midnight. He looked around for the black Silverado, but there were three of them parked on the street. Jim mumbled to himself, “Well, fuck me. Three goddamn trucks, and I can’t run around looking at license plates to see if one of them is John’s.” He got out of the car and walked up to the front door and rang the bell. He did it several more times until a light and then the porch light came on as well. Margo Dell peeked through the thin white curtains that covered the glass windows of the front door. She had a sleepy look in her eyes and then an alarmed one, seeing the Sheriff of Los Angeles County standing on her doorstep. She unlocked the deadbolt and opened the door. She had a sheer robe on covering her just below the waist.

Jim looked at her and asked, “Mrs. Margo Dell?” “Yes.” “My name is Sheriff Jim O’Brian. I wondered if I might have a word with you.” She wiped the sleep from her eyes, invited Jim into the kitchen, and asked, “What can I do for you, Sheriff?” “I was looking for your husband, Mrs. Dell. Is he here?” She got a surprised look on her face and said, “No, actually, he’s not here. He was supposed to meet me at ten last night. He said he had a surprise for me.” “And he’s not here?” “No…I got home, and the house was set up in a very romantic way, but Brad was nowhere to be found.”

"Does he disappear like this a lot? You don't seem too concerned." Margo reached for a coffee pot and asked Jim if he would like a cup of coffee. He told her yes, and she started to prepare the coffee while answering, "Oh...Brad does pull his little vanishing acts two or three days a week. Sometimes it's school-related. He is on a bi-weekly rotation along with the police at the high school he teaches at for alarm calls. He might have gone out on one of those, and if so, he will call me when he is cleared to leave the school."

"Does he leave without telling you where he was going?" "He wasn't here when I got home, and he didn't leave a note or message for me, which is unusual, but he will turn up." She poured two cups of coffee and handed one to Jim. He took a sip, and she leaned against the counter, her robe revealing her nude figure underneath it, and asked while taking a sip of her coffee, "So, what do you want with my husband at this hour?" Jim took a drink of the coffee and said, "I got a tip that he might have some information on the death of one of the students at his school, and I wanted to talk with him." Margo laughed and reached for her purse on the counter and pulled out a pack of cigarettes and offered one to Jim. He shook his head and pulled his own from his top left pocket and flipped his Zippo open and lit Margo's cigarette as well as his own. There was silence between them for several minutes. Jim couldn't take his eyes off of Margo's supple breasts under the nightgown and her beautiful long black hair and dark eyes.

She was flirting with him, and he knew it. She leaned over the island in the middle of the kitchen where Jim was standing drinking his coffee and allowed her robe to fall open and her breasts to rest on the counter and said, "Why on earth would you want to come out in the middle of the night to interview my husband, Sheriff? I'm his lawyer. I would strongly advise him not to answer questions under these circumstances." Jim took a deep drag off the cigarette and said, "I'm not really here for your husband, Mrs. Dell." "Please, call me Margo. If you're not here for Brad, then who are you here for?"

"You, Margo. I'm here for you." She took a long drag off the cigarette in her hand and then stubbed it out in the kitchen sink. "Well, if that's the case, Sheriff, you can have me." She said it in a low sultry voice and opened her robe and put her arms around Jim's neck. He reached down and put his hands on her ass and grabbed it tight. "You're a very beautiful woman, Margo. I wish I were here on a social call, but I have reason to believe that your life is in danger." She nuzzled her face into Jim's neck and said, "My husband is gay, Sheriff. He doesn't think I know it, but I do. I haven't had sex in two years. I see that you have a ring on your finger. Does your wife fulfill all your needs?" Jim pulled away and said, "I love my wife. I'm sorry that your husband is in the closet and even more sorry that I am not the cheating type because you're gorgeous, and any man would be lucky to have you. Right now, however, I must insist that you get some clothing and come with me."

Margo stepped back and asked, "And where are we going? Am I under arrest? Are you taking me downtown?" Jim looked at his watch. It was half past twelve. "No. I'm taking you with me into protective custody. I know that you work for the public defender's office in Van Nuys. I know you know the law, but right now your life is in jeopardy, and it is my job to protect you. I'm going to ask you to trust me, and I will keep you safe." Margo asked Jim to follow her, and he did…right into her bedroom where she stripped off the robe and stood nude in front of the closet. She grabbed a small bag and asked, "How long will I be away?" "I would not think more than a night or two." "And where will I be staying?" There was a long pause as Margo put some clothing into her bag and then put on a pair of sweatpants and a sweatshirt.

"You will stay with me and my wife at our home." Margo turned and smiled at Jim, the soft light from the closet flashed in her eyes, and she said, "Well, well. There is hope of getting laid. I know your wife, Barbara, well. She will be quite shocked to see me, but that could be a good thing for you." She followed Jim out the front door and locked up the house. He led her to his vehicle, and once she was seated, he made a call from his cell phone while standing outside the car. The phone was ringing, and Jim was trying to control a raging hard-on.

"Swenson." "I have Margo Dell. I'm taking her to my home for safe keeping." "Good. There's been a change of plans. I have to pay a visit to one of Dell's colleagues, so he will remain with the Eagle." Jim had a thoughtful look on his face and asked, "You don't have Dell with you, do you?" "I have him. He's just not in my truck. I need to grab Trent Hameln." Jim stepped away from the car and asked in a low voice, "Who the fuck is that?" John laughed on the other end of the line, "You'll learn that soon enough. You will be happy to know that Mrs. Dell was very, very close friends with Jill Makin. You remember Jill, don't you Jim?"

A smile grew across Jim's face, and he asked, "How close?" "Oh, now Jim…if I tell you that it will take away the surprise you're going to get when you get home. I know that Barbara knows Margo Dell well." "How the hell do you know so fuckin' much, John?" There was a slight laugh, and John said, "I know what I know. Look, you are going to have the rest of the night before I will be calling on you, so use it well. In the meantime…who runs TOR in your office?"

"You mean the 'onion?'" "Yes." "Fuck, man, I don't know shit. That's all part of our cybercrimes unit. Why?" "Find out who's running it and have them start a search using the names of the four kids we are seeking." "What the fuck for?" "I don't have time to explain…it's deep web stuff, Jim…hell is about to come to dinner at a local high school unless you and I figure out what's happening."

Jim hung up the phone and called his office and passed the information on to his cybercrimes unit. He got in the car and drove off headed for Malibu and home. Margo was sitting in the seat next to him, smoking a cigarette and chatting him up. Based on the conversation, Jim knew she had no idea where her husband was, and he was not about to get into that.

The only sound was the crashing of the waves outside the bedroom window where Chris lay wide awake staring up at the ceiling. He was nude and laying on top of the blankets, his eyes in a dead stare through the glints of moonlight that entered the room off the sea outside his window. There was a light tap on his bedroom door. He answered it with his head sticking out the door. Karen was standing on the other side. “I can’t sleep,” she said and asked Chris if he could. He shook his head. “Neither can I.”

“Want to talk?” said Karen. She was dressed in a pair of skimpy shorts and a short cut tank top. “Let me put some clothes on.” Karen giggled and said, “I’m a big girl, Chris. If you’re comfortable in the nude, I’m a doctor. It’s no big mystery. You all have the same equipment.” He grabbed a robe off the end of his bed and his cell phone and walked out into the lightly lit hall. He followed Karen to the kitchen, and she poured a glass of juice, offering him one. He nodded, and she poured some for him and then the two sat down in the breakfast nook staring at each other.

“Where’s Sara?” Chris asked. “I would assume asleep, but then again who knows. She and John keep strange hours.” “Have you seen or heard from John?” Karen asked. “No…I’m getting stressed out, too. I fucked up, and a young girl’s dead.” Chris took a drink of his juice, and Karen asked, “Has anyone ever told you how I came to know John and Sara?” Chris shook his head, and Karen said, “Let me tell you a story.”

It was two thirty a.m. when Jerry and Tim pulled up to Jerry’s house. They looked around, and all was quiet. Tim asked, “Is there anyone home?” Jerry shook his head. “Then let’s get in and get your shit before anyone else does.” They got out of the car, and Jerry walked up to the front door, unlocked it, and walked in. The house was dark, and Jerry made his way to his bedroom and turned on the light. Tim was behind him when he hit the lights, and both men were surprised to see Jerry’s father sitting in a corner of the room with a Glock nine millimeter hand gun in his lap. Tim froze as did Jerry.

His father looked on at the two young men and said, "I found this gun in your dresser, loaded and everything. Where did you get it?" Jerry walked slowly over to his bed, and Tim stepped into the room. Jerry's father pointed at him and said, "You…get into the room where I can see you." Tim walked in and stood next to the closet door. Charles Pinskey, thick in the middle and nearly completely bald, was sitting in Jerry's leather recliner, and the three men were separated by at least thirty feet. Charles looked at Jerry and asked, "Where did you get the gun, son?" "I got it from Tim." Tim shot him a dirty look, and Charles asked, "Is that true?" He nodded slowly, and Charles asked, "And where did you get the gun?"

"My father, sir. He has an extensive collection of weapons, and we both are gun enthusiasts." Charles nodded and said, "You and Jerry also seem to be killing enthusiasts." Tim froze, and Jerry moved slowly and sat down on his bed and asked, "What are you talking about, Dad?" "You know damn well what I'm talking about. I hacked your laptop and got into TOR and looked at your posts." Tim wasn't surprised. Charles was a computer expert and worked for one of the largest antivirus software companies in the country.

Charles continued, "I hacked your chat boards in TOR. You killed Brian Donaldson the other night, and now you're planning a mass killing at your school. What the hell are you thinking, son? I know what Donaldson and that rat pack of thugs he hung out with did to you and Tim as well as Mark and Alan. We discussed it. I understand you wanted revenge on Brian, and I would never say a word about it to anyone, but you boys are plotting to kill a bunch of innocent kids. What the hell for…what has a whole school done to you that would deserve that type of reaction?"

Jerry was sitting near the head of his bed and laid down on his pillow and said, "You wouldn't understand, Dad. You could never understand." "Try me." Tim was leaning against a double set of mirrored closet doors watching Charles's every move. "Look, Dad, even if I could explain it in a way that you would understand, you still wouldn't. You are past all the high school bullshit. You're a nerd who has a calling, and you're a nerd who has a high powered job in the tech world. You're a code breaker, man. You don't live in the same world that we live in where the tormenting never ends, and everyone hates you. You hacked my TOR account, so I'm sure before you found that you hacked my regular computer. Did you read the posts and threats on my social media pages?" Charles nodded.

"How about it, Dad. Would you like to be living that nightmare? It's not the world you grew up in. I know you work to protect systems and security, but you're not getting hate email and social media posts constantly from anonymous accounts from people you go to school with who are telling you to kill yourself because you're a worthless nerd. You don't constantly have to look over your shoulder to see where the next attack is coming from. Hiding in alleys and walking in groups to hide from would-be attackers. It's a whole new world, Dad, and I'm living in it. The rest of our group is living in it. There are only two options as we see it: do what the pretty and popular people want us to do and kill ourselves or fight back, and that means with brutal and deadly force. I choose to make examples of the pretty people and let them suffer the way we have suffered."

Tim looked on, and Charles said, "You know that I can't let you do that, right? You know that I have to do the most difficult thing a parent would ever have to do. I have to report you and your friends to the police." Jerry moved his hands quickly and came up with a small shotgun from under his pillow. He shot his father in the chest before he could move, and Jerry rushed him and took the Glock from his lap. Charles looked at him in shock and horror. Tim stood silent, watching the whole situation unfold. "Who have you told, Dad?" Charles was struggling for breath, and Tim could see into Charles's chest, blood squirting out onto the chair. "No one, son. I just hacked your system an hour ago."

Jerry pulled back on the Glock and said raising it to his father's head, "Good. Dad, I'm sorry for this, but there is no other way." And with those words, he put a bullet in his father's head then grabbed his laptop and other equipment and said to Tim, "Let's get the fuck out of here.

There's no doubt that someone heard the shots." They ran across the yard to Tim's car as the sound of sirens could be heard in the distance. Jerry said, "Fuck, man. I know who made the call, and I know that she's sitting in her front room window hiding behind the curtains with her little note pad with your license plate number on it, Tim." Jerry put the Glock in his waistband and ran two doors down from his house.

Tim watched as Jerry pulled the Glock and yelled, "You nosy fuckin' cunt," and emptied the gun into the house. Tim heard breaking glass and saw Jerry reach into the darkness and then come running back to the car screaming for him to start it. Jerry jumped in as the sirens grew closer, and they sped off into the night. Jerry handed Tim a little note pad and said, "You see what I mean…that's your license plate number on that piece of paper. All that the cops will find will be my old man with two gunshot wounds and that old fuckin' bitty, who's been a thorn in my side since I was a little kid, with two bullets in her gray haired fuckin' head."

"This is going way too far, Jerry. You just killed your own fuckin' father. Do you know what that's called in psychology circles? Patricide. Mother fuckin' patricide. When the fuckin' cops see that you killed your old man, they'll know you will kill anyone. You just heaped a world of hurt on all of us." Jerry smiled and put the gun to Tim's head and said, "Well, if you believe that then you won't do anything to piss me off, right?" Tim nodded as a chill came over him.

Jerry said, "This plan is going to happen with or without you, Tim. They are going to pay for what they have done." Tim drove on down Balboa Boulevard heading back to Northridge, his eyes on the road and Jerry holding a gun to his head.

CHAPTER ELEVEN

"I know there is hope in the darkness."

In the fourteen hundred block of Valley Vista Boulevard in Sherman Oaks, it was half past three, and Trent Hameln was out walking his German shepherd, Roscoe. He had told his wife he was going to take a quick quiet walk as he couldn't sleep. He and Becky had lived in the upper middle class neighborhood for two decades. She was a middle school teacher who taught special education. Trent never understood how she could put up with the "little pieces of shit' as he had just told her after backhanding her upside the head for back talking him before taking off for his walk. Becky Hameln was lying on the floor, unconscious, with a small pool of blood trickling from her right eye.

"Dumb ass cunt. After twenty years together, you would think that you would have learned never to sass me." Trent was talking to himself and Roscoe under his breath as he rounded the corner a few doors down from his home when he saw a tall dark figure hidden in half darkness near a street light. Roscoe started barking and tugging on his chain and choker collar. Trent crossed the street away from the figure all the while trying to calm Roscoe down. "It's okay, boy, relax. One of the neighbors probably had one of their costume parties, and it's a late departure for one of their guests." He continued walking on past the figure that stood not moving in the darkness. Trent made his way a few more houses down when he realized that the figure was moving on the other side of the street behind him. He pulled his cell phone from his sweatpants and held his thumb over the red panic button that would call a 911 operator. He walked a few more steps then turned around in a confrontational pose only to see that the figure was gone.

Roscoe was eerily quiet and was standing at full attention looking straight ahead. Trent turned back around and said to the dog, "Jesus Christ. I'm scaring the hell out of myself, Roscoe. Relax. There's no one there." He took two more steps before he felt a sharp sting in the back of his neck. He released the leash, and Roscoe took off into the darkness, barking and growling as he went. Trent slumped on two plastic trash cans in front of one of his neighbor's homes. He looked around, but there was no one there. He was starting to black out as he pressed the red button on his cell phone, and a pair of headlights approached him. He waved a weak arm, and the vehicle stopped in front of him.

"Help me…please help me." He felt a strong pair of arms grab him and lift his two hundred and fifty pound six foot tall body into the air and then felt the soft touch of leather on his face before he blacked out. The Eagle pulled the passenger door closed and took off down the street headed for his lair. Roscoe was running behind the truck, barking, and continued until the Eagle turned the corner headed for the freeway and his lair.

Jim and Margo walked through the doors of his house at a quarter to three. The lights on the patio were on, and Margo and Jim walked through the living room and out to the deck where Barbara was sitting, drinking a glass of scotch with her back to them. Jim had not uttered a word when Barbara said, "Good evening, Margo." Jim stood in stunned silence. "Good morning, Barb. How have you been?" "I have been doing very well thank you. How about you?" "I've had better mornings; I have been taken into protective custody by your husband who thinks that I'm in danger." Barbara stood up and walked past the two on her way to the wet bar in the living room.

"If Jimmy has taken you, you can be sure that you are in danger. He doesn't get involved in cases like this unless he has some very good intelligence, isn't that right Jimmy?" Jim just looked at Barbara in her white robe putting ice in three glasses and then pouring scotch in them from a decanter. Jim said, "Yeah…she is in fuckin' danger. I don't know just what the danger is, but I have been given good intelligence that Margo Dell needs protecting." Barbara turned to the two of them and handed each a glass of scotch. Margo took hers and dropped her bag on a love seat next to the sliding doors. Jim watched as the two women walked out onto the deck and sat down on two lounge chairs and started chatting. Jim took his glass and joined them.

Barbara was asking Margo, "So…has Brad come out of the closet?" Margo shook her head, taking a cigarette out of the pack that Barbara had on the table. She looked at Jim and said, "Can I have a light, please?" Jim pulled out his Zippo and lit her cigarette. Barbara grabbed one as well, and Jim lit it then took one for himself. There were a few moments of silence, and Margo asked Barbara, "Do you mind if I take a dip in your pool?" Barbara laughed and said, "Not at all, kid. Strip and swim." Margo stripped off the sweats and put the cigarette into an ashtray on the table and jumped into the water.

Jim got up and sat down on the lounge chair next to Barbara and asked, "You two know each other?" Barbara took a deep drag off her cigarette and said, "Oh, yes, Margo and I know each other very, very well." "Would you care to fuckin' enlighten me?" Barbara laughed as Margo got to the steps of the pool and started to walk out and asked Jim for a towel. He pulled one off the back of Barbara's chair and handed it to her. "So…what's the topic of conversation?" Margo asked, picking up her cigarette and sipping her scotch. "Oh, Jimmy wants' me to 'fuckin' enlighten' him as to how we know each other." Margo looked over at the two of them sitting and said, "So, you want to tell him or should I?"

Barbara stood up and said, "I'm going to bet that you haven't had a good fucking in at least a year, maybe more." Margo said, "I haven't had a 'good fucking' in five years since I married Brad." Barbara said, "Well, come on. If there's one thing that my Jimmy does well, it's fucking, and the two of us will give you one hell of a fucking, isn't that right Jimmy?" Jim stood smoking his cigarette and staring at the two women, now both nude and walking toward his bedroom. He stubbed out the cigarette and then slapped himself hard on the side of the face. "Well, I'm not dreaming because that hurt like hell." He heard Barbara calling him, and he walked on into the bedroom where the two women undressed him and began working on his cock.

He felt Margo's hungry arms pulling him down to the bed, and he groped in the darkness for a few minutes until the three were entwined with one another, and the sweat was dripping off his face onto Margo's nude back.

The Eagle had placed Trent on a gurney next to the bodies of Mark Rubio and Brad Dell. He tied Trent down and prepared his instruments of torture. Hameln was still out cold, and the Eagle left him in the operating room tied to the gurney as he moved into the conference room. He opened his laptop and logged in with his fingerprint and retinal ID then pulled up TOR and started to work on a program to find Jerry Pinskey, Tim Elliott, Alan Marks, and Debbie Atwater.

John started a program that only he and three others at the Bureau knew how to operate. He began to do SEO with the names and the plots that he had learned about, allowing the program to run its own auto sequencing and searches looking for the three men and the girl. Sara coughed under her breath, and John looked over to see her standing in the conference room doorway and asked, "So, did you get Vickie Delgato's killer?" John shook his head. "Do you know where he is?" He shook his head again. She walked in and put her hand on his shoulder and bent down and kissed the back of his neck. "You will, sweetheart, you will." John kissed her bare arm and said, "I hope the hell so, Sara… because if I don't there's going to be a lot of dead students and teachers."

Sara pulled on his arm and asked, "How many guests does the Eagle have?" "Three but only one is alive." "How long will the live one be out?" "A few hours." Sara took his hand and said, "Then come with me. You need some sleep if only for a few hours." John followed Sara as she held his hand and pulled him out of the lair and toward their bedroom. They both noticed that the light was on in the kitchen, and they walked over to see Karen and Chris sitting at the table in the breakfast nook. Chris looked up at John and Sara with tears in his eyes. Karen was sitting across from him and looked over with tears in hers as well.

Sara said, "It's three thirty in the morning. I take it you two can't sleep?" They both shook their heads. John looked at Karen and asked, "Are you taking Chris for a walk down nightmare lane?" Karen nodded fast, trying to hold back tears. John stepped into the kitchen and walked over to her and put his hand on her shoulder. She put her hand on top of John's, and he leaned down and kissed her on the cheek. He whispered into her ear, "You're safe now. The black angel has you." She smiled a big smile and looked over into John's piercing blue eyes and whispered, "I…know…" She was choking back tears and whispered, "I'm trying to help Chris understand that he can't save everyone. I know that first hand." John stroked Karen's hair. He was misty and noticed Sara was, too.

"Well, you two kids try and finish up your conversation before the sun rises, okay?" They nodded, and John went to walk out with Sara but stopped. He turned around and looked at Chris who could not make eye contact with him and said, "You fucked up, and a young girl is dead. You can beat yourself up over it, or you can learn from it. You have to grow a thick skin if you're going to be in the business of justice. I'm not angry with you. You were just trying to do your job.

Listen to what Karen has to say about her own life and experiences. She knows what you're going through, and she is good counsel." Chris nodded and said, "All of the reassurance in the world doesn't change what happened last night. A girl is still dead, and I am the reason."

John looked at him and said, "No… you made a mistake, but you weren't the one who chose to take that girl's life. A sick twisted guy decided to do that. Now take all of that anger and misery and put it to good use and help me find this guy and his cohorts before a lot more innocent men, women, and children die at their hands." Chris nodded, and John and Sara left.

Sara looked at him as they got into bed and asked, "Do you think that Chris has what it takes to be an agent?" John laid down beside her in the darkness and took a hold of her hand and drew a deep breath and said, "I not only think he has what it takes to be a great agent, I think he has the capability of meting out justice in his own way and in the footsteps of the Iron Eagle." Sara put her head on John's shoulder, and the two fell fast asleep.

Karen and Chris were still sitting in the kitchen at four thirty. She said, "I don't know about you, but I'm sleepy." Chris nodded, and Karen said, "We are only going to get a few hours before the world comes crashing in on us." Chris nodded and said, "Yes…but now that I know the type of world you came out of, and who saved you, I know there is hope in the darkness." Karen smiled and took Chris's hand and said, "I've never been with a man I cared about, but I care about you. If you feel the same about me, then I would like to sleep in your bed this morning." Chris leaned in and gave Karen a gentle kiss that turned warm and passionate. He picked her up and carried her to his bedroom and gently kicked the door closed behind them. She felt the power in his arms and said, "I have a feeling this is the beginning of a hell of a love affair!" Chris nodded as he removed Karen's shorts and shirt, and the two became one in the early morning fog that was rolling over the house on the edge of the sea.

Jim was awakened by his cell phone and rolled over to pick it up off the night stand. He looked at the clock, and it was six fifteen a.m. He grabbed it and laid back down on the pillow and said, "What?" "Good morning, Sheriff!" Jim recognized the voice right away. "Riggs, what the fuck are you so chipper about at this hour of the morning?" "I'm standing at a crime scene that I think that you and Agent Swenson will find interesting." Jim sat up on his elbows with the phone to his ear and said, "Hang the fuck on…I'm in bed." Jim got up and walked out onto the deck overlooking the pool and the sea and sat down in one of the patio chairs, grabbed a cigarette from a pack on the table, lit it and asked, "You got a homicide?"

"Yep, and it's none other than Charles Pinskey." Jim took a hit of the cigarette and asked, "Charles Pinskey? The father of Jerry Pinskey?" "Yep, and he's dead." "Well, no fuckin' shit, Sherlock. Would you be calling me if he wasn't?" "Man, you're on fire this morning, Jim…he's either dead or he has some new type of skull to brain air conditioning system though he has no pulse." Jim let out a laugh and asked, "Suicide?" "Homicide, Jim. Homicide. Pinskey got his head blown off, and based on my review of the scene, it was his kid who killed him."

"How the fuck would you know that?" "Because the body is in a chair in his kid's room, and the room is pretty messed up." Jim laughed, putting out the cigarette, "If there's one thing I know about teens is their rooms are never neat and clean. What's the address?" Jim wrote it down and asked, "Is Jade Morgan on scene?" "No, but I have a call in to her, so she should be here shortly." "Okay, Riggs, hold down the fort. John and I will get there as fast as we can." Jim quickly called John.

"Swenson." John's voice was bright and awake. "Jesus, man, do you ever sleep?" "I was asleep. Now I'm awake again because of you. What's up?" "I just got a call from Riggs. He has a crime scene at the Pinskey home." "Did the kid off himself?" "Nope. Looks like the kid offed his old man." "Shit…what's the address?" John was typing it into his phone as Jim gave it to him. "Is Jade on scene?" "Not yet. Riggs said she is on her way." "Okay…I'm on my way out of here. Did you get to Margo Dell last night?" Jim looked back into the bedroom where Margo and Barbara was sleeping nude on his bed. "Um…yeah…you could say that."

"What do you mean, 'You could say that?'" "I have her in protective custody." John stood up and was walking into the bathroom. "You were supposed to get her out of the house while the Eagle did his work." "I got her out of the house alright. Did the Eagle do his work?" "It's not all finished yet. What the hell did you tell her?" "That she was in danger, and that I was there to protect her." "And she went with you without a fight?" "Oh yeah…seems Barbara and Margo know each other really fuckin' well…they were lovers at one point when Barb met Jill."

"Okay…so what does that have to do with anything?" "Nothing for you…it meant some hot sex for me with Margo and Barbara, and now I'm getting run out of the house for the Pinskey murder. I want to get me more of that." John started laughing and said, "You can die happy. You finally got your threesome. Was it everything you imagined it would be?" Jim sighed, "Better. Way mother fuckin' better, man. What a morning." John walked into the bathroom and said, "I'll see you on scene," and hung up. Sara called out to him and asked, "Is everything all right?" "I have to go to a crime scene. Can you make sure that the Eagle's guest naps until he returns?" Sara let out a big yawn and asked, "How long do you want him out?" "Give him a slow drip of sedation. It will most likely be a chunk of the day." "Yeah…no problem." Sara put on her robe and headed for the lair while John brushed his teeth and dressed.

They met in the kitchen, and she said, "Okay, the Eagle's guest is in a low grade coma." John was taking a swig of a Coke Zero and asked, "Was he awake when you walked in?" "Yes, sir, he was. He gave me a little lip, and I set an IV and put him to sleep." "His wife will report him missing any time now." Sara smiled, pulling the coffee pot from its stand, "So…we know where he is, and that's what matters." John kissed her on the cheek and walked down to Chris's room to get him up to the crime scene. He opened Chris's bedroom door to see him and Karen asleep in each other's arms.

"Hey lover boy!" Chris opened one eye and then shot up in the bed. He moved so fast he threw Karen on the floor. "What, um…sorry John…um." Chris's eyes were glazed over, and he looked around the bed but didn't see Karen. "Oh shit, that was a dream." Karen's voice rose from the side of Chris's bed and said, "No, Chris, it wasn't a dream, and you just gave me a hell of a wakeup call." Chris shot out of bed and grabbed Karen off the floor and put her back on the bed. Her nude body was lying on top of his bed sheets, and John looked at Chris and said, "Let's go, man. We have a murder scene, and it's the father of the guy who killed your witness last night." Karen just laid on the bed looking at the two men as Chris ran around putting on clothes.

He leaned down on the bed and kissed her on the lips and asked, "Can I buy you dinner tonight?" She stretched out her arms in a yawn and said, "You're damn right you're buying me dinner. I put out, and I got no meal or smooth talking before it." Chris said he would see her at six, and she said okay. John looked on and asked Karen, "You put out without a date?" "What can I say, John. I'm a hopeless romantic." "No, you're a horny young woman who hasn't had sex in a while." "So shoot me…" John turned to leave the room with Chris behind him, and Karen called out, "Chris is an amazing lover, John." John never looked back. "How the hell would you know, Karen. He's your first." "Not true, not true at all. I had some boyfriends in college." John was shaking his head as the two men walked out the front door. He called back to Karen and said, "I don't want to know. I will try to have your new…friend back for dinner."

Sara called out to John as she ran across the foyer, "Hey Agent Swenson, you want this laptop?" Sara had closed it, and John asked, "Did you shut it down?" "No…it has an interesting screen though… it also looked like it had some data hits." Chris was looking at John and Sara as they spoke. She handed him the case and asked, "TOR huh? What are you looking for in the deep web?" John's face became grave, "Killers, Sara. Savage, young, cold-blooded killers." Sara turned to walk back into the house and said, "Well, I think you have some interesting information on that screen, Agent Swenson."

Chris and John got into his truck, and Chris asked, "Are you mad at me?" John smiled and said, "No…Karen could do a lot worse." Chris smiled, and John said, "Open my laptop. Sara thinks I made some hits on these guys on TOR." Chris opened the case, and there were four names. "You have hits on Jerry Pinskey, Alan Marks, Tim Elliott, and Deborah Atwater." John smiled and said, "Read me what the reports say." Chris started reading as John hit the gas and headed out onto PCH for the Pinskey home.

CHAPTER TWELVE

"He painted this uncanvassed wall with his father's brains."

"Twenty four, seventy two, fifty eight, forty five. This will allow you access to Anchor Store five at Northridge Mall. This will only allow you to unset the internal alarm. The mall cameras are on a separate circuit, and you can't crosscut it, or you'll set the whole place alight with police, fire, and paramedics. I've had two storage containers set near the store's rear entrance, and they have all of the contents you ordered for your pipe bombs and hand grenades. Payment has been received; good luck gentlemen." Tim was reading the message on his TOR instant message board from user 'terror55.' It was half past seven, and Jerry and Alan were asleep on the floor in the living room. Debbie was asleep with her head on his lap, and he was sitting on a sofa that had not been sat on in a really, really long time. He looked around the room; it was as if he had been sent back in time. The whole home décor was late nineteen seventies, and he felt like he was sitting in a mausoleum.

Jerry was asleep on the floor on the other side of the room, and Tim looked on at him and whispered, "You would think that you didn't have a care in the world. You killed your father, you sick fuck." Tim's voice roused Debbie who slowly sat up and looked at him and then his watch and asked, "Where are we, and what are we doing?" Tim smiled and said, "Just give it a second, and it will all come flooding back to you, I promise." Tim saw the look on Deb's face as the horror of the past several days grew across it. "There's no way out now, is there?" He shook his head solemnly and said, "No…not a chance… it's all in motion now, Deb. We have to see it through."

Jerry roused as did Alan, and Jerry sat up and asked, "Have either one of you heard from Mark?" Tim and Alan just shook their heads. Jerry said, "Fuck…I bet you that little faggot blew his nerve and told Dell the plan. Shit…now we are in even deeper." Tim closed his laptop and said, "Jerry, we are already in too deep. There is no turning back from here. I received the information to enter the store, and 'terror55' has had two storage containers with pipe bomb manufacturing goods delivered to the site. We have access, so we need to get over there ASAP and set up the first round of kill zones."

Jerry nodded and said, "Well, we need some damn food. Alan… you're the least known of all of us." Jerry handed him a hundred dollar bill and said, "Go to the store and get us some food. Shit we can microwave or eat out of a box. We don't have a lot of time to waste." Alan took the bill and left. Tim stood up and stretched his legs and said, "You know the cops are crawling all over your house and your dead neighbor's house right now." "Yeah, yeah…what the fuck. They won't even know it was me. They will chalk it up to a random act of violence."

Debbie laughed, and Jerry asked, "Did I say something funny, princess?" "Yeah, actually you did. You don't think that the cops and the feds aren't going to place you at the scene of the crime?" "No…why? Do you?" "Oh yeah!" "And just how will they do that?" Tim handed Jerry his tablet. The screen was black, and Tim told him to press the middle of the screen. When he did, it was as if he was watching some brutal murder movie. Jerry was watching himself killing his father and then a split screen of him killing the neighbor. "Where the fuck did you get this?" Tim laughed, "Well, it wasn't very difficult. Several of the kids in your neighborhood found the footage when they learned of the kills and posted them to live TV vision on the net, and it's all over TOR, so everyone gets to enjoy watching your father and neighbor getting killed."

Jerry watched the footage a few more times then handed the tablet back to Tim. "I forgot about the cameras in the house and the neighborhood." Debbie laughed a little and said, "Obviously…you're an Internet sensation. You did some major killing." Jerry just stared at her saying nothing, waiting for Alan and the food.

The Pinskey home and neighborhood was overrun with law enforcement and media. They had local LAPD, LA County Sheriff, FBI, homeland security, DEA as well as the ATF. Jim was standing in between the Pinskey home and Marilyn Pruitt's home. Her bullet-riddled front door was open, and her body sprawled out on the foyer floor. John and Chris pulled up, and John jumped out of the truck with Chris on his heels, heading for Jim. "This scene has plenty of attention," John said, watching the bustling people. He saw Jade out of the corner of his eye as she was walking out of the Pruitt house with a bag of evidence. Jade saw them and asked, "You guys just show up?" John nodded. Jim looked at her and said, "No…my ass has been here for nearly two hours. You see those fuckin' news crews over there?" He pointed a finger in the direction of yellow crime scene tape covering the street and keeping the press at bay. "Yeah," Jade said casually. "I get to go over there and try to placate them with an explanation for the double homicide that happened here this morning. Care to join me?"

Jim pulled a cigarette out of his top left pocket and lit it, snapping his Zippo shut. Jade walked over and took the cigarette out of his mouth, took a quick hit off it, then kissed him on the cheek and said,

"Not at all…you are so good with the media. I would never want to take that away from you." She put the cigarette back in Jim's mouth and looked at John and Chris and asked, "So what are you two brain surgeons up to?" "Who's the corpse?"

"That, John, is Mrs. Marilyn Pruitt, a widow and long time neighbor of Charles and Jerry Pinskey." John looked on at the house and damage and said, "Let me guess…Jerry and Ms. Pruitt didn't get along?" Jade laughed and said, "Wow. You are on fire this morning. Was it the bullet-riddled house or the proximity to the Pinskey home that gave it away?" Chris let out a laugh, which drew a frown from both John and Jim. John said, "Okay, smartass, if you keep up the comedy skits, I'm going to have to make you give a statement to the media…I know that you love the media almost as much as Jim does." Jade raised her hands in the air and said, "Sorry, I'm sorry. The old bird over there is a widow who liked Charles but not the son. I haven't talked to anyone yet, but I have heard interviews with a few of the other neighbors who said that she and the kid's old man had a thing, and that the kid hated her. I guess, Jerry, that's the son of Charles if I didn't mention it..." Jade was staring at Chris when she said it, "Jerry must have decided not to just ice Dad but girlfriend and favorite neighbor, too."

"Do you have an estimated TOD?" John asked. "I don't have to estimate. I can tell you exactly based on the security footage that caught both killings. Dad at three twenty-two a.m. and Mrs. Pruitt over there at three thirty-three a.m." "Who's got the footage?" Jade laughed and said, "The fuckin' world. Someone posted it online before the cops were even on scene." John and Chris walked over to the Pinskey home with Jade on their heels. Jim shook his head and pressed his heel into the cigarette he threw on the ground and said, "It's going to be a long fuckin' morning." The four walked into the Pinskey home and into Jerry's bedroom. Jade said, "The kid is an artist." She pointed to the walls covered in canvas paintings all signed by Jerry. "Yeah…and he is pretty damn good," John said as he walked over to Charles's body. He leaned down, looking into the cold dead eyes of Charles Pinskey staring back at him and said, "He painted this uncanvassed wall with his father's brains."

Chris looked at the three of them and asked, "Is it always like this?" Jim asked what he meant. "I mean, are you guys like this on every crime scene? I would think there should be a little respect for the dead." That drew a loud and hard laugh from Jim who looked at Chris and said, "You're fuckin' kidding me, right? Our respect for the dead is to untangle a crime scene and bring the killer to justice. Fuck, kid, I really don't know if police work is for you." Jade looked at Chris and smiled a sad smile and said, "Levity, Chris. It's what keeps all of us sane in these situations, and while Jim is a sick twisted fuck, he's right. The way we serve the dead is by finding their killers." John leaned down and looked at the two bullet wounds and said, "Patricide is serious business, folks. If this kid will kill his own father, he will kill anyone."

"Well, I'm not a cop. I'm an assistant coroner in training, but I agree." Chris looked up to see Jessica Holmes standing near him in a blue coat with gloves on and an evidence bag. John smiled as did Jim, and Jade said, "What you got there, kid?" "Some of the buckshot that the kid put into his old man's chest. I'm amazed he lived long enough to have his head blown off." Chris looked down at what remained of Pinskey's head and said, "Jesus, he blew half of his head off." Jim let out a laugh and said, "Yeah, Riggs said either Pinskey had found a new way to air condition his brain or he was dead."

"But he's dead, isn't he, you cold fuck?" Jim turned to see Lieutenant Riggs McEllen looking over their shoulders. Jim nodded and shook his hand. John asked, "Do you have access to the footage of the killings?" "The world has access; we are working with some of the major search engines to get it taken down. Follow me." Riggs walked out into the living room where there was a laptop sitting on a wet bar. He pressed the enter key, and the screen was in split screen mode, and they watched the video. John looked at Riggs and asked, "No audio?" "Well, the cameras have microphones on them, but we can't make out what's being said. You can hear the shots. The kid never raised his voice." John looked at the clear HD video of Jerry Pinskey shooting his father, and as he watched, he froze the frame after the second gun shot.

Jim asked, "What the fuck, John. We need to look at it a few more times." John took a pen out of his pocket and pointed to the screen of Jerry shooting his father and said, "Jerry Pinskey isn't alone." Jim and Chris looked hard at the frozen frame, and Jim saw it before Chris did. "Son of a fuckin' bitch. There's a shadow behind Pinskey as he's shooting. Fuck, John, how do you pick this shit up? I don't think anyone would have caught it." Chris looked hard and said, "I don't know, John. I think that might be a shadow cast from that dresser next to the bedroom door." John shook his head and said, "The man is sitting in the chair. He has a weapon. It looks like a Glock, and he never moves to shoot. Also, if you watch the film from the start, Pinskey motions in his son's direction after his son is in the bedroom. Someone else is in this room. Someone else was involved in the killing."

Chris and Jim stepped back, and John called out to the crowded living room and asked, "Does anyone know what Charles Pinskey did for a living?" Riggs was over with another officer and called to John, "The guy was a computer nerd for an antivirus company." John stepped back into the bedroom and looked hard at the scene. There were two small desks, and he could make out several small dust rings and told Jade, "Make sure that this room gets photographed before it gets dusted for prints." Jade asked why. "At least two, maybe three, computers were on these two tables. I think that Charles found out what his kid was up to and was laying in wait for him. I also think that Pinskey kid was coming home to get the equipment because it had the secret that he and some friends are working really, really hard to keep. I think Dad hacked the kid's computers and was hoping to get an explanation. He might have even been going to call the cops. That's why the kid shot him."

Chris and Jim were back watching the video, and Chris called out and said, "I can make out the voices, and it sounds like Dad asks son some pointed questions about school, and the kid is talking about bullying and cyberbullying before he goes medieval on his old man." Jim took out a cigarette and said, "The kid shot his pop with the gun that was in his father's lap for the second shot…that's what created that Jackson Pollock look on the wall. Perhaps the kid is going in a new artistic direction." That got an eyeroll from everyone in the room.

Jim walked out to the front yard and lit up while looking over at the media circus on the street. John said, "I'm taking the films back to the lab to see if I can dissect what's on them." Jim took a deep drag and said, "I heard the conversation pretty well. I can tell you what they were talking about. The father hacked the kid's computer and discovered a plot to kill a lot of people. The kid was cool through the whole conversation then pulled what looked like a sawed off shotgun out from under his pillow, shot his old man in the chest, then took the gun from his lap and blew his head off."

"You heard all of that?" Chris asked. "Yeah…he's plotting something to do with his school. I agree with John that there was someone else with the Pinskey kid when he killed his father. What I didn't get was who, what, when, or where the kid is planning to kill next." John asked Chris to grab his laptop from the truck, and as Chris walked away John said, "Pinskey is the ring leader in a plot to kill kids at his school. I don't know for sure when, but I have picked up some intel that it might be during homecoming." Jim looked at John and asked, "And just how did you get this information?" John smiled, and Jim said, "Great. I'm going to have an Iron Eagle mess on my hands, too." Chris came back with the laptop, and John showed the tracers that had been picked up on Pinskey and his friends. Jim looked at the messages and said, "Well, I see the FBI is putting my tax dollars to good use. So you have some encrypted messages. None of them talk about a school shooting or killing."

John said, "If you understand text speak and IM language, you can glean a lot from these messages, and that's exactly what they are talking about." "Okay, smartass, so where and when?" John looked at the screen blankly and said, "I don't know yet, but I will." He closed the laptop, and Jim said, "Well, I have to go and play meet the press. Anyone want to step up with me and poke the bear?" John shook his head, and Chris just looked on. Jim was dressed in his full uniform and said as he started for the press, "Just a few more months and this nightmare will be over, and I'm so fuckin' retired." Jim grumbled on as he walked away, and Chris looked at John and asked, "So how are we going to find these killers?" John snapped the laptop shut and said, "By becoming one of them."

Alan got back with the food for everyone pretty quickly, and they all ate like refugees as they plotted the work they had to do at the store. Jerry said, "Alan, you have some unfinished business with Johnny Belk." Alan nodded with his mouth full. Jerry asked Tim, "Jesus, what day is it?" "Sunday." "Fuck, man, it feels like it's been a week. Alan, do you know where Johnny would be today?" "Yeah, his old man has a tree trimming and landscape business, so he is most likely working for him." "That narrows it the fuck down. Do you know how to find out where they're working?" Jerry and Tim were standing over his shoulder as he brought up the website for the business. 'Belk Landscaping' popped up on Alan's screen, and he picked up his cell phone and called the business line. A man answered, and Alan pretended he was a customer looking for a bid. There was back and forth, and Alan could hear the sound of heavy equipment in the background. He had Johnny's father, Ron, on the line, and Belk said, "Look, sir, I'm on a big job in Chatsworth for the next several days, and I don't have a free man to send out to give you an estimate. If you will give me your number, I will call you when the job is done."

Alan asked, "You are not far from my property. How about I come out and talk to you?" "Well…the job is not finished. I don't want you to get the wrong idea about our work." "I won't. It will give me an idea of what you and your men do." "Yeah, okay. We are working at the Chatsworth Reservoir at the intersection of Plummer and Valley Circle Boulevard. You can't miss us. We have about ten big covered trucks, some feller bunchers, and wood chippers, too. We are doing some clean up for the city from the fires a few years ago; the reservoir has a ton of debris, so we have been hired to clear it."

Alan thanked him and asked what would be a good time to come out. "Well, we are working today until six p.m. Any time is fine. Just ask any of the guys on the scene for me, and I will be happy to talk to you." Alan thanked him and hung up. Debbie looked at him and said, "That was really smooth, Alan. So what are you going to do? Johnny is no doubt working with his father. He bitches about it all week long. I've heard him with the others talking about having to work on the weekends." Alan closed the laptop and shrugged his shoulders and said, "I don't know. I will go out there and see if I can cause Johnny to have an industrial accident."

Jerry looked at him and said, "That dude will kick your ass if he sees you and so will his workers." "Then I better make sure he doesn't see me, huh?" Jerry laughed and said, "Well, it's your turn to take out your assailant, so do your thing. I'm going over to Dell's house and see if I can find out what happened to Mark and maybe get some of Dell's wife's pussy. Have any of you ever seen Margo Dell? She's a fuckin' babe, man." Tim said, "Yeah, I saw her about a year ago in Van Nuys Court when I was there over shit with Brian and Rocky over a restraining order. She's a fox, but there is no way she's going to let you into her pants." "Who said I'm going to give her a choice? Maybe I'll get lucky and Mark and Brad will be out, and I can grab her at home and rape her ass!"

Debbie stood up and said, "You're way over the line, Jerry." He stood up and made a sudden move in Debbie's direction but was blocked by Tim and Alan. "I am going to rape your ass, too, Debbie. These two aren't always going to be around to protect you. You fucked us over with the cops with your big mouth. I'm going to put it to good use on my cock." Debbie spit at him and said in a cold and threatening voice, "Go ahead, big guy, you try it. I'll take your cock in my mouth. I'll take the goddamn thing all the way down my throat, and then I'll bite the fuckin' thing off and swallow it!" The two stood staring each other down as Alan said, "Okay, Debbie, you're coming with me. Put on those hot shorts of yours and a skimpy top. You can be the distraction while I try to take out Johnny."

Alan logged back on his computer and opened TOR. He posted a couple of messages in some chat rooms on executions explaining where he was going and who his target was. He got back several instant responses and two that had photographs of the landscape trucks on the job in Chatsworth. Tim was looking over his shoulder reading the responses. Alan wrote a few things on a piece of paper while Debbie was off changing and then logged off. Tim said, "Really fuckin' creative advice you just got." "Hey, that's what the chat rooms are for, man." Jerry was looking at Debbie as she reappeared from the bedroom in almost no clothing. He licked his lips. She was braless in a low-cut top; her nipples were hard, and she was wearing a pair of skin tight terrycloth shorts.

Alan asked, "Are you going to stare at Deb, or did you have something to say?" Jerry looked away and said, "Just remember the cops use TOR, too, and they could be monitoring your chat room antics." "Yeah, well, I'm encrypted, so no one knows it's me." Jerry laughed and said, "Yeah, but they know where you're going, dumbass, and what you're going to do. It won't take much to put two and two together." Alan just shook his head as he waved for Debbie to follow him, and they walked out the door headed for Chatsworth.

CHAPTER THIRTEEN

"It's never too late to
turn from murder."

TOR was open on John's laptop, and he was monitoring several chat feeds that were going back and forth in rooms that Jim's team had discovered. He was about to close up when he caught some chat between four people talking about a killing in Chatsworth. He looked down at the screen then at his watch; it was eleven a.m. John and Chris had only been back in the office for about a half hour, and John asked Chris, "Did they get you a car?" Chris nodded. "Okay, I want you to go over to Brad Dell's home and interview him." "About what?" "I have it on good authority that he knows something about what this Pinskey kid and the others are doing. Ask him about Donaldson and see if he has any idea who could have killed him." Chris looked at John and asked, "Don't you think someone has already done that?" "I'm sure they have, but I want you to do it from the federal level." Chris shrugged and said, "You're the boss."

John waited for him to leave the building and then told his secretary he would be out, and if anyone needed him to call his cell. He took off for Chatsworth, saying to himself, "I might not know which one of you is going to Chatsworth to make a kill, but you won't be hard to identify." He threw a duffle bag onto the passenger side floor and drove down Wilshire to the 405 Freeway and headed into the San Fernando Valley.

The sound of chainsaws, heavy equipment, and wood chippers assaulted Alan and Debbie's senses as they parked their car on a dirt road across from the job site on Valley Circle in Chatsworth. Alan told her to stay put while he ran over to the site, but she asked, "Don't you think that Johnny will see you?" Alan nodded, saying, "He might see me, but I doubt he's going to try and start shit with me while he's on the job with his father." "So much for the element of surprise," Debbie said, shaking her head. Alan ran across the street and ducked down behind two large trucks looking for his target. He could see the front grill of his car parked off the road and Debbie leaning across the hood like a pinup girl. There were some whistles and catcalls as the men stared at her sheer t-shirt and short shorts.

Alan whispered under his breath, "Fuck, if Johnny sees you, he's going to know I'm here." A food truck pulled up on Valley Circle and parked and honked its amusing horn, and the men began to break away from their work and head for lunch. The truck was parked not ten feet from where Debbie was flaunting her assets, and Alan tried to keep an eye on her as well as look for Johnny.

The black Silverado pulled into a brushy area where Plummer Avenue turns into Valley Circle. The foliage was heavy and once the truck parked, it could not be seen from the street. The Eagle pulled on his mask. He was well equipped to take down the assailant whoever it might be. A silver flash off of a chrome bumper caught his eye. The Eagle saw the side of a silver car parked in the weeds across from the job site, and he worked his way around behind some boulders, trees, and scrub brush until he was behind the car. The rear license plate was in plain view, and he burned the numbers into his mind then made his way back to his truck. The silver laptop was on the passenger seat, and the clock showed twelve noon. He watched as the workers were getting their food and chatting up a young girl. He opened the laptop and within seconds Alan Marks's name popped up on the screen with all of his information, including his driver's license photograph. The Eagle was surprised to see that Alan had no rap sheet. Unlike Pinskey and Elliott who had histories with law enforcement, Alan had nothing. The Eagle ran the plates off one of the work trucks and all but one were registered to Belk Landscaping.

There was a small Toyota pickup that was owned by John Belk, and when the Eagle ran his information he got a really good picture of a really, really bad guy. Johnny had a rap sheet a mile long, and he had several outstanding warrants, two were for assault and battery. John Belk's photograph from his license was of a shaved headed white male with multiple tattoos on his neck and a tear drop under his left eye. "So, John boy wants to act like a gangbanger," the Eagle said, looking at the photograph. "It doesn't work. He looks ridiculous." The Eagle looked up from his computer to see John Belk walking across the street to the food truck. He watched as Belk got some food wrapped in yellow paper and then walked over to the girl now sitting up on the hood of Alan's car. The Eagle looked around for Alan Marks, but he was nowhere to be seen. He made his way back over to the car and leaned against a large boulder that the car was backed up against and listened.

"You're not pretty, but you have a hell of a body, bitch," Johnny said as he walked over to the car and Debbie. "You like my body, Johnny?" Debbie slid off the hood and turned around and wiggled her ass at him. The other guys from his work crew let out laughter and catcalls as Johnny walked over and ran his hands over Debbie's ass. He had a burrito in his mouth that he was holding with his teeth, so he could feel Deb up and said with the food in his mouth, "Oh fuck yeah, bitch. I want me some of that." He pushed his pelvis against her and started dry humping her. Debbie turned around and saw Alan running deeper into the job site. No one saw him as they were distracted…or so she thought.

Debbie looked at Johnny and said, "The last time you touched me was with Brian, Rocky, and Billy. Do you remember that, Johnny?" A smile broke across Belk's face, and he moved in close so Debbie could feel and smell the stink of his breath and said, "Oh yeah baby…I remember. We fucked you ten ways from Sunday that night. Hell, it took me two days to get your shit off the end of my cock. It was worth it, though. We thanked Greta and Beth for inviting you to our little pig party. You were really, really good." Debbie shuddered, and Johnny smiled and said, "Yeah baby…you know you want it again. How about I take you to the back of this car and fuck you?"

The guys were all whooping and hollering, which finally caught the attention of Johnny's father who walked across the street and asked, "What the fuck is going on over here?" Johnny backed down and got very contrite, "Oh nothing, Dad. This is Debbie Atwater. She's a friend from school." Ron Belk looked at her with disgust in his eyes and said, "I've heard of you, you little tramp, and now seeing you, I see that you are everything that John has said you are. What the fuck are you doing here?" Ron asked with frustration in his voice. "I came out to get a little sun, that's all, sir. I saw Johnny, and we started talking." The guys started to break up and head back to work, and Ron looked at Johnny and said, "You…get your ass back to work." Johnny skulked off as his father told Debbie, "You stay away from my boy, you little slut. I know your kind, and it's your kind of slutty and disgusting antics that end up with good boys like my son ending up in bad situations."

Ron walked back to his truck, looking back at Debbie two or three times. When he was back across the street, Debbie moved to the edge of the street and lifted up her t-shirt to give him a shot of her braless triple D breasts, which brought a round of applause from the workers. Ron yelled at the men, and Debbie then walked back over to the car and laid spread eagle on the hood in the sunlight.

Alan had seen where Johnny had been working and had slipped in behind some stacked lumber and fallen trees and waited for him to come back. Johnny was sitting on the tailgate of his truck finishing his lunch and watching Debbie who was taunting him. She had taken off all of her clothes and was lying on the roof of Alan's car. She called out to Johnny and said, "I know none of you is going to call the cops on me for indecent exposure." There were more cat calls and whooping, but Johnny kept his head down since his old man was staring at him from two trucks over. He finished his food and saw his father walk back into the reservoir.

Once he was out of sight, Johnny ran across the street and grabbed Debbie by the hair and said, "Where the fuck is Alan? This is his car." Debbie cried out a little, and Johnny said, "Don't make a sound, bitch. I might not be able to rape you right now, but I can sure as hell cut you and fuck you up…now, where is Alan?" Debbie spoke calmly, "At home. He let me borrow his car because mine is in the shop. I was driving out to the beach and saw your father's trucks and thought I would tease the guys. I had no idea you were here." Johnny smashed Debbie's head down onto the hood of the car, and a small trickle of blood started to flow from her nose. Johnny pressed the side of her face and said, "Why don't I believe you? Why do I think that Alan is out there on my job site waiting to jump me?" There was a moment of silence, and Johnny released her and said, "I have a hundred pounds on the fucker. I hope you're lying. I hope that fucker is out there. I fucked him up the ass with Brian and the guys at camp. If I find him, I will do it again right here on this job. If he thinks I'm going to end up like Brian and Rocky, he has another thing coming."

He drug Debbie off the hood of the car and threw her nude body down on the ground. He looked around to see if there was anyone who could see him, but there was no one. He smiled and said, "Bend over the hood, bitch. I'm going to get some more of your shit on my dick!" Debbie was pulling herself up by the front grill on the car and said,

"No!" Johnny hauled back and slapped her across the face. "Bend over!" He pulled a razor knife from his work pants and pushed up the razor blade. "You can take it up the ass, or you can have my initials carved into your fuckin' face. Choose."

The Eagle had heard all he needed and was about to pounce on Johnny when Ron Belk's voice began echoing through the air, calling Johnny's name. He had Debbie pressed face forward with her ass in the air against the car when he heard his old man. "Oh, mother fucker, if he sees me with you, I will catch a wrath of shit." Johnny had pulled his pants and underwear down while he had been beating on Debbie, and he struggled to get them up and on to run back across the street. While she was distracted with everything that was happening, the Eagle moved silently behind her and slid a transponder under Alan's car. He heard the click of the magnet against the frame and then moved back behind the rock. He pulled out a small tablet from his body armor and pressed a button and the blip of the GPS tracker now on Alan's car lit up as a green light. He put the tablet back and slid back into the cover and then across the street to where Belk's company was clearing trees.

Alan was sitting under a large California Live Oak watching and waiting for Johnny. He had grabbed a sizable piece of wood that had been laying next to a wood chipper and held it in his hand like a bat. He heard some brush moving behind him and turned to see a coyote run out of the thick brush and off into the dry reservoir. Alan looked back over to where Johnny had been when he felt a sharp blow to the side of his head. Johnny Belk stood over Alan, now bleeding and said, "You came out here to kill me, you little fuck. Debbie was just a distraction, so you could get to me. Son of a bitch. It was you who killed Brian and Rocky?" Alan shook his dizzy head and said, "I had nothing to do with their deaths. Those were carried out by their other enemies." "So what the fuck are you doing out here in the middle of a Sunday afternoon, huh?" Alan started to get to his feet, and Johnny pushed him back down, "Answer the goddamn question, Alan…what…the fuck…are you doing here?" Alan's eyes started to tear up, and he said, "I came to kill you, you son of a bitch. I came out here to kill your lying raping ass." Johnny started laughing and picked Alan up and threw him across the yard and into the back of the wood chipper.

"You came to kill me?" Alan nodded. Johnny let out a giant laugh and said, "Well, the joke's on you, asshole. I'm going to literally fuck you up. Take off your pants and underwear and bend over that rock." Johnny was pointing to a small shelf shaped rock outcropping next to the area of land he had been clearing. Alan stood up and said, "Not this time. You're going to die today, Johnny. Right here, right now. It's time for some justice." Johnny lunged for Alan, but he moved and Johnny ended up hitting his head on the side of the chipper. He pulled his arm back and was about to hit Alan when the two heard the chipper fire up. Johnny looked over at the control center, but there was no one there.

Johnny looked at Alan and said, "So, you got that little cunt out here with you, huh. What? You thought you would knock me out and throw me into the chipper?" Alan shook his head slowly. His eyes were as big as saucers, and he was staring behind Johnny, not at him. Johnny yelled over the roar of the chipper motor, "GET YOUR GODDAMN PANTS OFF. I WANT SOME OF YOUR SHIT ON MY COCK!" Alan just shook his head. Johnny moved to grab him but was stopped in his tracks. He had the look of a man stuck, and he twirled around to see a huge figure dressed all in black holding onto his jacket.

"Who the fuck are you supposed to be?" Johnny said in a defiant voice. The Eagle picked Johnny up by the throat and pulled him close to his masked face and said, "I'm justice, you piece of shit. You might also have heard of me. I'm the Iron Eagle." Alan looked at Johnny dangling in the air. There was yellow liquid running out of the bottom of Johnny's pants, and the Eagle threw him into the chipper, pressed the blade release lever, and the blades began spinning at high RPMs. Johnny was lying near the edge of the hopper that fed into the machine, and he screamed as two colored bandanas that he had on his pants got grabbed. In a matter of seconds, there was nothing but a cloud of blood and bone fragments being thrown out the exit shoot and onto the ground.

The Eagle turned and grabbed Alan and carried him by the back of his neck out of the area and to a clump of trees about a hundred yards from the chipper and threw him on the ground. Alan looked up at the giant man and asked, "Who are you, and why did you do that?" "I'm the Iron Eagle, and Johnny Belk needed to be killed. He could not be reformed. He would just keep getting more and more violent until I would end up taking him out." Alan started to cry and said, "Please don't kill me." The Eagle knelt down next to Alan and said, "Now that's all going to depend on you, Mr. Marks."

"How do you know my name?" "I know everything there is to know. You and your friends are planning to kill a lot of people." Alan said nothing, but the Eagle said, "I know your plot, and it will not succeed. If you and your friends continue down your current path, I will kill you all. You've gotten your revenge on John Belk. The score is settled. He got what he deserved. Now go back to your friends. They have settled their scores with all but one person. I know what happened to you all, and I'm not going to punish you for the punishing crimes against your aggressors, but if you continue down this road to kill innocents, then I will have no choice but to kill you all. Your friend, Mark Rubio, is dead, as is Brad Dell. If you don't want to end up like Johnny over there, or worse, turn back now." The Eagle started to walk away, and Alan said, "What if I can't stop it? What if it is too late and already in motion?" The Eagle turned back to him and said, "It's never too late to turn from murder. It's never too late to do the right thing. You have your whole life ahead of you. I would hate for you to end up one more victim of the Iron Eagle because you were too foolish to turn back."

Alan asked, "If I can stop this, I will try, but I don't think I can. I will step out of the situation, but the planning and the movements have started. How will you know when we move?" The Eagle leaned in close and said, "That's for me to know, and you not to find out." With that, the Eagle disappeared into the thick brush around the reservoir, and

Alan got up and ran back to his car where Debbie was sitting with the window down and her feet out the passenger window. He sat down next to her, and he saw her bruised face and bloodied nose and asked, "What the fuck happened to you?" "Johnny Belk happened to me. What the hell happened to you?" "The same." "So…" Debbie asked in a serious manner, "Is he dead?" Alan nodded and said, "Oh yeah…he's dead all right." "What did you do with his body?" Debbie asked, her silken soft legs still sticking out the passenger window. "Well…let's just say that he won't be identifiable." She pulled her feet out of the window and put them on the floor. Alan started the car and pulled out onto Valley Circle headed back to Plummer Avenue and Topanga Canyon Boulevard to head to the 118 Freeway and Northridge. They were both quiet for several minutes. As they turned onto the 118 Eastbound Debbie asked, "What the fuck happened back there?" "The Iron Eagle happened back there." Debbie's face lost all color, and she asked hesitatingly, "What do you mean?" "I mean Johnny got the drop on me and was kicking the shit out of me. He ordered me to strip, so he could rape me."

"How does the Iron Eagle fit in that picture?" "One minute I was about to pull my pants down and take it again, and the next this huge man in black stepped up, grabbed Johnny, told him he knew all of the things he had done wrong, and threw him into one of the industrial wood chippers." "Did he say anything else?" Debbie asked, staring at him. "Yeah…he said he knows our plot, and if we don't turn from it, he will kill all of us." He said, "We get a pass on those we killed who'd done us wrong, but our plan to kill innocent people will not succeed, and if we keep on down this road he will kill us." Debbie sat silent as they exited the freeway at Osborn Street. She looked at Alan and said, "There is no way the Eagle could know our plan." "Well…you might not think so, but I came face to face with him, and he claims to know the whole thing."

They pulled up in front of the house where Jerry and Tim were. It was half past two p.m. when she asked, "Are you going to tell Jerry and Tim?" Alan sat for a few seconds and said, "I don't know. What do you think?" Debbie smiled and said, "Even if you told them, they wouldn't believe you. Jerry is too far gone. He's not going to stop unless he kills everyone or gets killed. Tim will think that it's a joke and not take you seriously, and Mark…well Mark…when he finally comes back, he will be more interested in the Eagle's looks than anything else." Alan said, "Mark is dead!" "What…how the hell do you know that?" "The Eagle told me. He didn't give any details. He just told me that Mark and Dell are dead." Debbie sat back in the car with tears running down her face looking at the house and then Alan with a look of desperation.

CHAPTER FOURTEEN

"...that's the kind of shit that once you tell it, you can't untell it."

Chris pulled up in front of the Dell home at a little before one p.m. He pulled out his ID and rang the bell a few times, but no one answered. He looked inside the side windows of the house, but there didn't seem to be anyone home. He called out, "FBI," and heard a crashing sound like glass breaking coming from the back of the house. Chris took off for the side of the house. There was a tall wooden gate that blocked the entrance to the yard, and Chris grabbed the top of it and pulled himself up and over with little effort. He turned the corner when he saw a tall lanky young man with a brick in his hand, and Chris went for his weapon but not before the guy threw the brick at him, striking him in the solar plexus. He went down like a rock and watched as his assailant ran for the back alley fence and leaped up and over.

He got to his feet, trying to both catch his breath and stop the pain from the blow. He made it to the alley in time to see a black Mustang racing off and quickly wrote down the plate number and ran back into the Dell yard to the source of the sound. The patio door had been broken out, and based on the blood and garment fragments, his assailant had jumped through the door from the inside. Chris pulled his service weapon and entered the house, identifying himself while looking for the Dells. After he had cleared the residence, he called John's cell phone.

"Swenson." "I'm at the Dell residence, and no one's here, but someone was. I think it was the Pinskey kid." "Did you grab him?" John asked. "No. He got the drop on me and threw a brick into my solar plexus. After that, he jumped through a rear sliding glass door and took off." "Did you get a good look at the assailant?" "Yeah, and I got a plate number." "Then your trip out to the house was helpful. Is Mrs. Dell there?" "No…there's no one here but me and my bruised chest and ego." John laughed and said, "Run the plate and tell me who it belongs to." Chris walked out to his car and typed the plate number into the computer. In a matter of seconds, the ID came back, and he said, "Mother fucker!" "What's wrong?" John asked. "I was right. The fuckin' car belongs to none other than Jerry Pinskey." John laughed again and said, "That guy is the bane of your existence." "Yeah…well I've got his address. I'm going after him."

John said, "Don't bother, Chris. He's not going to be at any address associated with that car. What make is it?" "Black Mustang. And how do you know that this guy won't be at any of the addresses on file?" "A hunch…meet me at Santiago's. I will call Jim. We need to talk. I have new information." Chris said okay and put the phone down and sat down in the driver's seat. Still in agony, he slammed his fist down on the steering wheel then started the car and said, "That's the last time, you mother fucker…I'm going to get your ass, Jerry Pinskey, and when I do, I'm going to kick the hell out of you. You're gonna…'trip' down a bunch of mother fuckin' stairs upon arrest." He drove off headed for the freeway and Santiago's.

Santiago's was quiet. Jim and Jade were sitting on the deck overlooking the sea having a few beers and a little lunch. Jade asked, "How long have you known that John is the Eagle?" Jim let out a little belly laugh and a burp and said, "From his first kill at Pendleton." Jade took a sip of her beer and looked out over the sea and asked, "Why didn't you turn him in? You're a goddamn police officer. He's a killer." "Why haven't you?" That caught Jade off guard, and she finished off the beer, and Jim cracked open another one and handed it to her as he took out a cigarette from his top left pocket and lit it with his Zippo. Jade took a deep swig off the beer and asked, "You want the truth?" Jim let out a laugh, "Oh, the fuckin' truth, Jade. I can see right through lies." "I'm madly in love with John." Jim was taking a drink of his beer when Jade said it, and he choked on it, and she jumped up and patted him on the back. Jim had his hands spread on the table, both choking and laughing with the cigarette between the fingers of his left hand. Jim responded while still choking, "You're in love with Swenson?" She nodded, and he asked, "Does HE KNOW THIS?" "Not directly…I mean, there's a certain sexual tension between us. I know he likes me. It's all stupid, Jim. Just forget that I said it."

Jim laughed and said, "I wish I fuckin' could, but that's the kind of shit that once you tell it, you can't untell it. Jesus! Does Sara know?" Jade took a swig of her beer and looked up at the sky as she answered, "Well…yeah." Jim laughed again and took a hit off his cigarette and asked, "And what does she have to say about it?" "It's just a joke between us. It's not something that we really talk about. Besides I have really poured my soul into Jessica Holmes. She is finishing up her first year of medical school, and she will spend the breaks working with me at my office." Jim took a drink of his beer and said, "That's one really, really smart girl. I have to tell you, to come off the streets with the things she has seen and been through and to be getting ready to be a second year medical student…that's a hell of a story." Jade smiled and said, "And she has you to thank for it." Jim threw a weak hand at her and said, "No, she has herself to thank for it. When I released her from my protection after we solved the Hollywood murders, she could have gone back to the street, but she didn't. She got with you, and if anyone is to be credited with saving the kid, it's you." Jade took a drink of her beer as Jim reached for his ringing cell phone.

"WHAT?" Jade jumped in her seat. "We need to meet and talk." John's voice was somber on the other end. "Yeah so…I'm at Santiago's with Jade. You want to meet me here with your protégé?" "Yeah, I'm en route as is Chris." "What…you two fuckin' butt buddies aren't together?" "No…he's on his way back from the Dell house. He got attacked by Jerry Pinskey when he went to talk to Margo." Jim laughed. "What the fuck, man? Margo is at my place with Barbara and has been since early this morning." "Yes, Jim, I know that. I sent him over there while I ran some…errands." "I see…and how did those fuckin' errands work out? Are the errands still breathing?" "One is. I have a good handle on the plot now. I know who the ring leader is and what's going to be a mass rampage on Rosedo High School."

Jim took a drink of his beer and said, "And you want to tell me about it?" "Yeah…you, Chris, and I need to talk. There's not much time. This thing is going to blow sky high, and I do mean that literally and figuratively." "Well, I'm just sitting here with Jade. We stopped off here after the Pinskey scene and the fun news conference and interviews I had to give. So come on down. Do you want me to send Jade away?" "No…she knows about the case, just not the gravity of it…she can stay. I will be there in five minutes. Chris might beat me. I don't know. He got hit in the solar plexus with a brick, so I'm sure he will be sore." Jim started laughing, "John, I know you think that Chris is cut out for police work, but I don't see it. The guy is most likely going to end up dead the way he's been going." "Don't say anything to him about it, okay? The kid has had a hell of a past few days."

Jim saw Chris walking in the front door of Santiago's as John spoke. "Yeah…what the fuck, just get your ass here. Jade and I have jobs to do, and Chris just walked in." Jim hung up, and he and Jade sat drinking their beers when Chris walked over to the table. He was walking a little slow and was favoring his midsection. Jim called out to Javier to get Chris a coke, but Chris waved him off and said, "I need a shot of tequila and a Corona." Jim let out a deep belly laugh as he put in the order for Chris. Jim said, "Javier, one shot of Patrón for my amigo and a Corona…" Jim took the last hit off his cigarette as the drinks came. Chris took the shot and chased it with a swallow of beer. He sat back in his chair, and a sense of calm came over him.

Jim looked at him and said, "Maybe there's hope for you yet. You're starting to drink like a cop…now if you could just keep from getting your ass kicked by the fuckin' bad guys we might get somewhere with you." John was within earshot when Jim said it and saw the empty shot glass and the beer. "That bad, huh?" Chris looked at John and said, "Oh mother fucker…yeah, it's that fuckin' bad." Jade laughed and said, "You will be fine, Chris, just keep taking deep breaths. I have to get going. You want to have dinner tonight?" Chris shook his head and said, "No thank you, Jade. I have other plans."

Jade looked at him crossly and said, "Don't tell me that you're seeing someone else?" John and Jim just looked away as Jade stood over Chris with her hands on her hips. "Yes, Jade. I'm sorry. I'm seeing someone else." She picked up her purse and put on her sunglasses. "Well, I know she's not a better fuck than me." John laughed under his breath as Jim said nothing. Jade looked at John and asked, "What's so funny, Mr. Swenson?" "Nothing…it's just that Chris has started seeing Karen." Jade's face dropped, and she looked at Chris and said, "You're dating a damn eighteen-year-old kid? You're ten years older than her. What the hell could you two possibly have in common?" Chris took another hit off the beer and said, "Surprisingly enough, more than you might think." Jade huffed and walked out of the bar.

John looked at the two men and said, "We have major trouble brewing. There's one more target of this small crew of killers, and then all hell is going to break loose on a school full of kids, and there's no way that I'm going to let it happen."

The black Mustang came screeching around the corner and into the driveway. Jerry parked in the garage and walked into the house where Tim, Alan, and Debbie were sitting. "Where the fuck is Mark?" Jerry cried. "Dead…Jerry. Mark and Dell are dead," Alan said in a monotone voice. "And how the fuck do you know that?" Alan stood up and paced the room. "I know that because I had my life saved this afternoon by the Iron Eagle." Jerry's face went sheet white, and he fell down into one of the kitchen chairs, taking deep breaths. He took a moment and then looked at Alan and said, "Explain it to me very slowly." Alan commenced to tell the whole story with Jerry hanging on his every word. When he finished, Tim looked at Jerry and said, "We are in way over our heads now. The Iron fuckin' Eagle knows our plot. He fuckin' killed Johnny Belk to save Alan, and the Eagle knows not only about Mark and Brad Dell, but he claims they are both dead. Am I the only one who can see that this ship is sinking?"

Jerry sat back in his chair and said, "Alan is still the cleanest of us all. He hasn't actually committed any crime." Debbie looked at Jerry and said, "He might not have pulled the trigger that killed Rocky, Greta, or Beth, or dropped the deadly modified plumb that killed Brian, but he knows all about it, and he is an accessory to all of the murders. He also knows about the plot for the school killings. He's not clean by a long shot." Jerry started pacing and said, "Well…the Eagle is sensitive to our situations. He understands. Hell, he even helped Alan kill Johnny. I'm sure he will understand how the rest of the plot must be carried out." Alan shook his head and said, "No, he won't understand. He made it very clear after he threw Johnny into the wood chipper."

Tim looked on as Jerry paced and said, "I need to take out Billy Stone, and we need to get the fuck out of Dodge." Jerry stopped pacing and looked at the rest of them and said, "No fuckin' way…we have plotted and planned this for nearly two years. We are not stopping now. Threats from this Iron Eagle guy or not. If he gets in our way, I will kill him myself." There was a round of laughter at the table, and Jerry sat back down with an angry look on his face. Tim said, "You think that you are any match for the Eagle? Come on, man…we have been getting revenge on bullies who did horrible things to us, and, hell, we have fucked up most of those. Mark got himself killed and most likely by the Eagle. You're going to kill the Iron Eagle, Jerry? The guy who stopped a terrorist plot to kill the president. The man who is known for hunting and killing other killers. No…Jerry…you're not…we are not. We go up against the Eagle … especially now that he has told Alan he knows our plot…and the only thing that's going to happen is the four of us will end up tortured and dead. I say we take out Stone and then get as far away from the valley as possible and start new lives somewhere else."

Debbie nodded as did Alan, but Jerry remained defiant. "I will not give up this cause because of some psycho killer. The plan is moving forward if I have to kill all of you and do it myself." Tim stood up and pulled a Glock from the back of his pants. He held it in Jerry's direction and said, "You have gone over the edge. You killed Brian, your own fuckin' father, and your neighbor, and now you dare to sit there and threaten us? Who the FUCK DO YOU THINK YOU ARE? I hate to break it to you, pal, but we are all you have. I think the Eagle's a badge. He knows what these guys did to us. I think he also knew about Dell, and I think he knows about Hameln, and if he knows about Hameln and the shit he's been doing to kids at the school for decades, it's only a matter of time before he ends up in the hands of the Eagle. I don't know what he knows or how much he knows, but he knows something, and in a case like ours anyone outside of our small group having a little knowledge will be a deadly thing for us. So…I'm taking Alan and Debbie with me, and we are going to get rid of Stone, and then we are going to keep on driving, never looking back and getting the hell out of California."

Jerry sat staring down the barrel of the gun pointed at him. "You know, Tim, there's a very, very strict rule when it comes to guns." Jerry was speaking as he stood up. "And what rule is that, Jerry?" Tim took his eyes off him for a fraction of a second…a fraction too long. Tim never heard the shot; he never felt the bullet that struck him under the right jaw and exited out the back of his head. Tim slumped over the table, and Debbie screamed at the gaping hole in Tim's head. His body slid down the table and onto the floor. Debbie was watching Tim dying and didn't see Alan running out of the room for the back door. She looked up, and the world was moving in slow motion. She saw Jerry turning and calling in a slow long drawl, "Baanng…baanng…you're…dead!" Deb saw a puff of blood come off of Alan's shoulder as he turned the corner into the kitchen and out of her sight. The chair that Jerry had been sitting in was hurling through the air behind him as he started to move in Alan's direction. He was calling out in words that Debbie didn't understand. Then in a flash, slow motion turned to high speed. She could hear several more gun shots as Jerry rounded the doorway into the kitchen.

Deb leaned down over Tim's lifeless body but could see nothing but death in his dilated eyes. She didn't realize it, but she was holding his blown open skull in her hands. She dropped him to the floor and ran out the front door of the house. She heard the sound of a car engine revving and the sound and smell of burnt rubber as Alan's silver car came careening across the front yard in her direction. She could see the passenger window was down, and she saw Jerry walking around the corner of the house across the driveway, firing as he walked. Debbie leaped in the direction of Alan's passenger window and landed face first in the passenger seat with her legs hanging out the window. She felt a sharp pain in her left calf but reached out for anything to hold onto as the car fishtailed down the street. And then, as fast as it had started, there was silence except for the hum of the engine. She felt the car moving down the street at great speed and off in the distance she could hear sirens.

CHAPTER FIFTEEN

"We can't save the foot.
We have to amputate."

Karen and Sara were in the doctor's lounge when they were paged to the ER. Karen looked at Sara and said, "Just once I would like to finish a meal here without getting run out for an emergency call." Sara smiled and said, "That's why it's called emergency medicine. We are here to handle emergencies…and an emergency isn't planned, kid." There were two quick pops, and Karen and Sara looked at each other and ran for the ER entrance hall. They came around the corner to see two hospital security guards lying face down on the floor with blood pooled around them and a tall thin man with a girl over his shoulder and a weapon in his hand.

"I need a goddamn doctor, and I need one now," Alan screamed with Debbie's limp body hanging over his shoulder. Karen and Sara walked slowly in his direction, and Karen called out and said, "We are doctors..." Alan looked around and pointed the gun at the two women and said, "I need you two to help my friend. She's bleeding really badly and needs help." Sara walked slowly in Alan's direction, and Karen followed and said, "Follow me." Alan pointed the gun at her as the staff in the halls took whatever cover they could find. "No tricks, bitch, or I will waste you and your kid." Sara pointed to a set of closed double doors and said, "No tricks. We are here to help you. Bring your friend this way." Sara and Karen were walking in front of Alan who was staggering a bit while following them into the ER and to a room with a gurney.

Karen said, "Lay her down here." Alan looked around and saw a few others hiding and said, "If anyone tries anything, these two are dead!" Alan was pointing the gun at Sara and Karen, and Karen said, "Sir… you're bleeding, and so is your friend. If you put her down, we can see what's wrong and try to help her and you." Alan laid Debbie on the gurney then moved over to the smoked glass door and closed it. He pointed the gun at them and said, "Help her! I'm fine." Debbie was breathing, but it was labored. Sara looked down to see that her right foot had been nearly blown off, and she was losing blood fast. "I need a tourniquet, stat." Karen opened a drawer and handed Sara a plastic kit. She ripped it open and wrapped the plastic kit around the wound and cinched it tight, and the bleeding stopped. "We need to type and cross her. We also need a surgical team in here and at least four units of O negative, stat."

Karen moved over to a phone on the wall, and Alan fired a shot near her head. "You're not calling the goddamn police. Get away from the phone." Karen turned around and said in a calm voice, "You nearly killed me…and it is only me and Doctor Swenson over there who are going to save your friend's life. She needs blood, or she will die, and she needs it now. Now, if you're her friend, put the gun down and help us save her. I have to call for other emergency doctors to help." Alan waved the gun and said, "Call, get the blood, get the staff you need, but make no mistakes. I see so much as a badge, and I'm going to kill the both of you. If my friend dies, I'm going to kill everyone in this damn hospital."

Karen picked up the phone while looking Alan in the eye and said, "This is Doctor Faber. We need four units of O negative blood, stat, in ER room two. We also need a crash cart and a surgical team." Karen hung up the line, and Alan slumped over the back of a chair, and she could see that he was shot in the shoulder. "We need to get your friend to an operating room." "No fuckin' way. You treat her here and now, or I swear the last thing you will hear will be silence." "We are going to need to have other people in the room, and we need them now."

"No…you two are the only ones who can work on my friend. Just get her to where I can take her and get out of here." Karen was still calm as Sara worked to stop the bleeding in Debbie's lower leg and foot. "What's your name?" Alan looked over at Karen and asked, "What the fuck does my name have to do with saving my friend? Ted…call me Ted." There was a knock on the ER door, and Alan swung wildly in the direction of the sound with his weapon. Sara cried out, "THAT IS THE EQUIPMENT AND MEDICINE WE NEED TO STABILIZE YOUR FRIEND. SHE IS IN SHOCK, AND IF WE DON'T GET HER BLOOD AND MEDICATIONS, SHE WILL DIE, AND IT WILL BE YOUR FAULT!"

Alan lowered the gun, and Karen ran to the door and opened it. Three other doctors rushed in. Alan was far enough away from Debbie and the door that no one could rush him, and he watched with the gun trained on Sara and Karen as they worked to save Debbie.

The emergency call went out to all law enforcement as John and Chris were driving back to the office on Wilshire. Chris was following John when the call came over the radio of a hostage situation at Northridge Hospital in the ER. Chris had looked away for a fraction of a second, and when he looked back, all he could see and hear were John's tail lights and the sound of his siren heading off into the distance on the 405 Freeway. Chris hit his siren and followed as they headed for the Roscoe exit.

Jim was racing down Roscoe with his radio in his hand barking out orders for a SWAT team and a hostage negotiator. He heard John's voice come over the radio calling for the very same thing. Jim threw the cigarette he was smoking out the driver's side window as he turned into the parking lot at Northridge. He jumped out of the cruiser like he was twenty and started barking orders to LAPD and sheriffs who were on scene.

"What's the fuckin' status in there?" Jim yelled. One of his deputies who was behind his car with his weapon drawn and trained on the front entrance to the ER said, "I don't know, sir; we have several reports of multiple hostages and several hospital security officers down." Jim worked his way over near the entrance where three other officers were on each side of the entrance to the ER.

"Has anyone made entrance?" The four officers shook their heads. Jim heard the screech of tires and looked over to see John and Chris parking behind his car and several other FBI vehicles and a truck with an armored assault vehicle on a trailer parking on Roscoe. They were blocking off the street as the men approached. Chris asked, "What do we know?" Jim looked on and said, "We don't know a goddamn thing. Supposedly multiple hostages, possibly several injured security officers and not much else." John looked around the area and asked, "Has anyone made entrance to the building?" Jim shook his head. John looked on and asked, "And no one has made contact with the hostage takers?" Jim shook his head.

Jim said, "I have ordered a hostage negotiator and my SWAT team. I know you did the same, John. That's all I know right this second. Is Sara on duty?" John nodded and Chris said, "So is Karen. She told me this morning she was working today." John looked down at his phone. It was half past four p.m. He said, "Time is not on our side here. I'm pretty sure that Sara and Karen are in the thick of this. Chris, follow me. I know a way in that won't draw attention." Jim said, "John…don't do it. You could end up getting everyone in there killed." John said nothing as he and Chris ran across the back part of the parking lot and over to the medical building adjacent to the emergency room. Jim cursed under his breath, "Fuck, John. You're going to get everyone in there killed."

Several cars pulled up on scene from Jim's office as well as FBI personnel. He saw Barry Ross stepping from one of the FBI vans. Barry had been a hostage negotiator for the Bureau for decades. Jim walked over to him, and Barry said, "Hello Jim. Where's John?" "I don't know, Barry, but you better make contact with whoever is in there because all hell's breaking loose, and it's going to get even worse." Barry patted him on the shoulder and said, "I will establish contact, and we will talk to whoever is in there. I will talk them down, I promise." Jim walked off in the direction of his own men and looked for John and Chris, but there was no sign of either of them.

Jerry was alone in the house. Tim's body was slumped against the wall where he had dragged it when he came in after shooting Alan and Debbie. He looked around and said to himself, "There's no way those two survived their gunshots. I got them both good. Now I need to finish this once and for all." He grabbed Tim's laptop and pulled up TOR and got the information he needed for the containers at Northridge Mall. The sirens were getting louder, and he took the laptop and two duffle bags that Tim had and ran out and threw them in his car. He fired up the Mustang and headed for the mall with a smaller arsenal of weaponry than he would have liked and was lighter on manpower, too.

He was cutting across Sherman Way headed for Tampa, which would take him to the mall and Anchor Store five. He looked at the clock on the dashboard; it was four thirty. "I can do this. I can set up the explosives. I have the time. With all of those pussies out of the way, I can finish this once and for all then jump a flight to Aruba and relax on a beach." Jerry's eyes were wild and crazy. "I can do this. I can make the kills and go to Aruba and live it up. There are no more cock suckers holding me down. I can do this." He sped off down Tampa to the mall, humming one of his favorite songs and smiling.

"We need to set a line. She's lost a lot of blood," Sara was calling out as two nurses were handing her an IV kit and hanging bags of blood on an IV pole. Debbie was lying there with her eyes closed. She was taking shallow breaths, and Alan saw it and asked, "What's happening to her?" Karen turned to him and said, "She's in shock. We are trying to save her life." Sara got the line set, but there was no other doctor in the room. She looked at Karen working down on Debbie's nearly amputated foot and said, "We can't save the foot. We have to amputate." Alan pointed the gun at Sara and said, "You're not amputating anything. You can put her foot back on. I've seen it on TV lots of times." Sara shook her head and said, "This isn't TV, kid. This is real life and real death. Your friend needs to have her foot amputated and the wound cauterized, or she will be dead in minutes."

Alan fell back against the wall and said, "She can't die…she has to have her foot. She dances…she's a beautiful dancer. You have to save her foot." Karen looked over at Alan and said, "We can only save your friend not her foot. Would she rather live and learn to dance with a prosthetic foot or would she rather be dead and never dance again?" Alan was displaying all the signs of blood loss, and his behavior got more erratic as he got weaker. "She's a dancer. She dances…I want to see her dance again." Alan was waving the gun around, and Karen said in a soft voice, "You will see her dance again…Ted." She smiled, and he smiled back at her, and she said, "Please don't wave around your gun. You might accidently hurt someone." Alan put the gun against his stomach and watched as Sara and Karen were working on Debbie and felt himself growing weaker and weaker.

CHAPTER SIXTEEN

"Ted, I promise you that the blood will by flying in this room in less than two minutes."

John and Chris had made it into the doctor's medical building of Northridge Hospital, and Chris asked, "Where the hell are we going?" John put his fingers to his lips as he saw two people hiding behind a hospital laundry hamper. He moved out into the open and behind the two, a man and a woman, and said in a whisper, "FBI." The two turned to see them and threw their arms in the air and fell onto the two men, crying. John pulled them into the office building entrance and asked, "What did you see?" The older white man in dress clothes said, "I didn't see anything. I heard a few loud pops, and then this woman ran me down, and we have been here behind this hamper. It feels like forever."

Chris was talking to the middle-aged Mexican woman in Spanish and after a few minutes of back and forth said, "She saw a man pull up in front of the ER entrance in a silver car. She says that he got out and took a girl from the passenger seat and walked into the ER and shot two security guards who were standing near the front door." Chris was listening as the woman in hospital cleaning clothes chattered on and then said, "She said that Dr. Swenson and Dr. Faber came around the corner and led the man with the girl into ER room two." John pulled out his tablet and activated its tracking software. The green GPS he had put on Alan's car on Valley Circle after their confrontation with Belk was blinking near the ER entrance. He looked at Chris and said, "Let's move." Chris asked, "Don't you want to know more?" "I don't need to. I know who it is, and I know what he is capable of."

Chris followed him down a long hallway in the hospital to a service closet. John picked the lock, and the two men got in. He said, "We have five or six minutes, and then this situation is going to go from bad to worse." Chris just looked at him as he took out his cell phone and dialed a number. There were a few moments of silence, and Chris could hear Jim's voice on John's phone. "Where are you?" Jim asked. "Chris and I are in a storage closet that has a large industrial vent that will drop us right into where the hostages are." "Well fuck me…do you know who the hostages are?" Jim asked. "Yes…Sara and Karen." "I pulled a trace on the plate of the silver car in front of the hospital entrance. It belongs to an eighteen-year-old named Alan Marks." There was a moment of silence, and John said, "Yes…I figured that out." "Do you know the kid?" "I met him briefly once," he said.

Jim said, "Well, word just came over that there has been a homicide at the old Watson house in Northridge, and the victim turns out to be the son of one of the nurses that works with Sara here at the hospital." John was unscrewing the vent cover and asked, "What's the guy's name?" "Tim Elliott. His mother's name is Linda. His old man is overseas and is a brigadier general named Gary Elliott. Anyone you know?" John said no as he climbed up into the vent and asked, "Who's my negotiator?" "Barry." "Hmm…has there been contact with Marks?" "We have made a few bull horn calls, but he has not responded. Barry has called into the ER. Sara and Karen are in room two. We have a line directly into the room, but no one is answering." John said, "There won't be an answer. Marks's cheese has slid off its cracker. He's going to massacre all of them." "How the hell could you possibly know that?" "I just know. I have maybe five minutes to get to him before he starts killing everything that moves."

John hung up the line, and he and Chris crawled through the vent passing over exam room one where John pushed down on one of the side panel outlets, and it gave way, and the steel grate almost fell to the floor. He grabbed it at the last second, and the two men dropped to the floor of the room, and he said, "Okay, here's where it's going to happen, and it's going to happen fast." "What's the plan?" Chris asked, looking into John's contemplative eyes. "For a few seconds just listen." John sent a text message to Sara. He could hear Sara's voice calling out instructions; he could also hear Marks getting belligerent and more threatening.

Sara was swapping out the third IV bag of blood as Debbie continued taking deep breaths, her eyes still closed. Sara felt her cell phone buzz in the pocket of her medical coat as Alan asked, "What's going on? What's happening to her?" "She needs more blood, Ted; I need to order more blood." "No, fuck no… you're keeping her down. You're not treating her because she's fine now. You're trying to trick me, thinking that it will save your lives. You're not using the damn phone." Karen said, "Look Ted…if we don't get more blood all of this will be for nothing, and your girlfriend is going to die." "She's not my damn girlfriend. She's my friend, and she's not going to die because you are going to save her. The longer she lives the longer all of you live."

Alan pointed the gun around the room. Three other doctors had joined in the fight to save Debbie's life, and now there were ten people in the cramped room all being kept at a good distance from Alan who was sweating profusely. He pulled off the sweatshirt that he was wearing, and he had at least ten extra capacity clips for his modified Glock spread around his waist band from front to back. Karen saw the lost look in Sara's eyes as Alan's shirt came off, and she knew that they weren't coming out of this alive. Sara said, "I can use my cell phone and send a message directly to the lab, and they will send up more blood for your friend, Ted. There's no way anyone on the outside will know." Alan pulled a fresh clip out of his pants, popped it in the weapon, pulled back on the mechanism, and loaded a shell into the barrel.

"That's just fine, doc, go ahead…text the lab and get the blood. If it's not here in two minutes, I will know you lied, and I will start blowing everyone in this hospital away starting with you." Sara pulled out her phone and saw the text from John. It simply read, "Exact location of gunman?" Sara typed in the location and then looked at Alan and said, "Ted, I promise you that the blood will by flying into this room in less than two minutes."

It was just five p.m., and the Northridge Mall was closed. There was no one around as Jerry pulled up outside the empty Anchor Store and parked next to the two containers. He entered the lock's combination, and the door unlocked. He smiled and opened the door and walked into the store. It was all dark. Jerry made his way to the main lights for the store and pressed a couple of buttons, and the two-level store lit up like a Christmas tree. He walked out into the main store, and it was decorated in his high school colors. It looked like someone had been working on the place for a month. He walked around looking at the decorations and lights in his school colors of white and blue and started laughing. "What the fuck…shit, man, someone has been busy." There was a table set up near the store entrance. The doors and windows were covered in paper, and he walked up and looked at a table that was all set up to receive guests.

He picked up a flyer that was on one of the tables along with a random name tag. The flyer read, "Come one, come all to the Regents Homecoming party of parties. Sunday the seventh at eight p.m." Jerry looked at his watch. It was five. He looked at the date on his watch, and it was the seventh. He started to laugh hysterically all the while heading back to the entrance where he had come in and said, "There is no fuckin' way I could get this damn lucky." He opened the two containers, and they were stocked to the hilt with plastic explosives, readymade pipe bombs, detonator pins, and a box of hand grenades as well as ten M-16s with an uncountable amount of ammunition. Jerry didn't miss a beat. He started grabbing case after case of material and hauled it into the store. He said to himself as he started to unpack the bombs, "Fuck, man. I really did need those fuckers. There is no way I can booby trap every entrance and exit to this place." He stood up and spread his skinny arms and said with a loud and excited laugh, "But I can sure as hell try. Come to Jerry, folks. It's going to be one bloody fuckin' homecoming!"

John's cell phone buzzed, and he read the message from Sara. He put his fingers to his lips and motioned for Chris to follow him. The two men entered the hallway next to the room. He could see the flashing lights of the police cars outside the building and heard Barry over a loud speaker calmly calling for the hostage taker to pick up the phone line, so they could talk. He got on the far end of the double doors into room two and Chris was on the other. John pressed his chest and legs hard to feel his full body armor in place. He looked at Chris and said, "Stay behind me when the shooting starts. It's not going to last long." With that, John pressed the automatic doors on ER room two and walked in with two modified nine millimeter handguns out and aimed.

Alan was leaning with the gun on his stomach when the doors to the room opened. He looked up to see a giant man with two weapons in his hands walking straight toward him. He got off three rounds, all striking the man in the chest, but they had no effect. The man kept moving, not flinching, just shooting. John fired three shots as well; the first struck Alan in the left thigh, the second in the right thigh, and the third in his right wrist, knocking the weapon out of his hand. John kept moving, not speaking as Alan hit the floor. Chris was behind him. John got over to

Alan, and he looked up at John and said, "I know you." John said, "I told you that this was going to happen. Where are the others?" "Dead except for Jerry Pinskey, and you know who he is, don't you?"

"Where is he?" "I would guess that he is at the Northridge Mall putting the finishing touches on the murder spree that you have been working to put down. The party for the school is tonight…and he will have to set it up alone." Alan let out a soft laugh as Debbie coughed and started to move her arms. Sara gave her a sedative. Debbie looked over at Alan lying on the floor in a pool of blood and said, "No…Alan, no!" "It's over, Deb…don't tell these fuckers anything…let Jerry finish off the massacre. I was wrong. I should have seen it through." And with those words Alan's pupils dilated, and his head fell back onto the cold concrete floor. Debbie was calling out his name as he died.

CHAPTER SEVENTEEN

"Poor old, Tim. All that work to collect weapons for this rampage."

It was half past seven, and several students from Rosedo High School had arrived to finish the final touches for the homecoming dance. Jeremy Levine was setting up the PA system and making sure that things were ready for the DJ who was due at any moment. Gabriel's Catering had two vans backed up to the store entrance, and several of the employees were setting up the food and snacks for the student body.

Cathy Hines was the coordinator of the whole event, and she had been working on it along with Mary Rubin throughout the summer. Cathy asked Mary, "Do you think we got the word out about the party to the whole student body?" Mary laughed and said, "Cathy, we got the word out to the whole San Fernando Valley." Cathy was setting up the last touches on the greeting table and said, "I don't know. There were a lot of people who thought that this was going to be on campus in the football stadium like previous years, and they think it's next Friday night." Mary shook her head and said, "The word is out there and

unless someone has been under a rock, they know that it's tonight."
"What's the head count?" Cathy asked. Mary pulled out her tablet and opened an Excel spreadsheet and said, "Shit, Cathy, we have over nine hundred students. Homecoming is open to everyone, so your guess is as good as mine as to the turn out. However, based on last year's numbers when we were juniors and running this, I think we can easily say half of the student body as well as all the faculty will show."

Cathy looked around and said, "Well if we are going to have near a thousand students and teachers, this is the perfect forum for it." Mary was following Cathy's eyes looking up at the open store building and the second floor railing that overlooked the lower floor. "It was really nice of the mall to donate this vacant store to us for our homecoming," Cathy said as she put out the sign-in sheet and made sure there were pens and blank name tags for everyone.

The last bomb had been set at the emergency exit, and Jerry was sitting with his back against the wall, sweat dripping down his face. He had changed into his black outfit and had several extra capacity magazines ready for his M-16 rifles. He had set guns in out of the way corners on all levels. He had also made it so he could move freely from section to section of the store, shooting his victims without being discovered. While looking at a slit of light coming through the semi-closed door of a janitorial closet, he said, "All you fuckers are going to die tonight, and by this time tomorrow my name and the names of those lost before this battle was raged will be known by every person in America and beyond."

He pulled back on the weapon to load it then set the safety. He also knew that school police would be monitoring the event, and there would be metal detectors as well as heightened security at the entrance to the dance. Jerry read over the manifest of all the weaponry he had in the store and said to himself quietly, "I will need to start rounds and take out cops as they start checking out the location. They will have the bulk of their detail at the entrances, and once the party starts, they will seal the entrances, so that no one can get in or out in case there is an incident like last year with the gang violence."

Jerry rose and took two Glocks from a case and loaded the clips and screwed on silencers. He laughed to himself and said, "Poor old, Tim. All that work to collect weapons for this rampage, and in the end the weapons I will be using came through the TOR black market." He stood up and headed for the closest exit to him to lay in wait for the first police detail to come through.

Sara and Karen were treating Debbie when Jade showed up with her team to deal with Alan's body. Debbie was feeling no pain after the amputation of her foot. Two surgeons had worked on her in the ER after John and Chris killed Alan as they were unable to move Debbie because she was part of an active crime scene and investigation. She was staring off at the ceiling, and John motioned for Sara to come close and whispered, "Do you have any SP-117 here?" She nodded, and he said, "We need to get this kid alone, and we need to get the drug in her and fast. Something horrible is about to happen." Jim walked over to the two of them and said, "Well, it looks like the Iron Eagle's not the only fuckin' guy who knows how to use a weapon or ambush someone."

Chris was standing off by himself when Karen walked over to him and asked if he was okay. He nodded and said, "Um…yeah…I have never been in on a kill before. That guy was going to kill you and Sara and everyone else in this room." "Hospital, Chris…that guy would have killed every person in this hospital if it had not been for you and John." "Yeah…I'm just starting to realize that what I learned in books and in controlled police environments doesn't prepare you for the real thing." Karen smiled and kissed his cheek and said, "Welcome to the real world of law enforcement. Your job is to swear an oath and protect people you don't even know, even if that means losing your own life."

Chris nodded slowly and saw Jim, John, and Sara talking off in a corner of the room. He saw Jade over near Alan's body, and everything was just moving. He said to Karen, "Everyone is going on about their business as if what just happened didn't happen." Karen smiled and said, "Life does not stop because someone dies, Chris. There's still a lot of police work to do, and John and Jim are planning their next move."

Jim and John looked over at Alan's bullet-riddled body, and Jim said, "If there is one thing I can say about you, you know how to leave a lasting fuckin' impression." John looked at Jim and said, "I need to get the girl out of here and to the lair." Jim pulled him out of the room and asked, "Just how the fuck are you going to do that without attracting a shitload of attention?" "You're going to do it!" Jim shook his head and said, "No…no way…not again. You just about got Chris killed this time, and you want me to interfere in an interdepartmental investigation?"

"Jim…I don't know how much time there is. Kids are going to die, a lot of kids, and I think that it's getting ready to happen right now!" Jim shook his head. John asked, "Do you want another rampage like we've seen in the past several years in schools, malls, movie theaters, and university campuses? Jim, what's about to happen here is going to take the body count for mass murder to a whole new level. I'm not talking about ten or twenty. I am talking about hundreds perhaps a thousand or more. We have the inside track here. I can stop it, but in order to do that I have to know when, where, how, and who." Jim took a cigarette out of his top left pocket and put it behind his ear and asked, "Okay, okay…how the fuck are we going to do this?" John said, "I'm going to have Sara put the girl into cardiac arrest and rush her out of the ER for surgery."

Jim laughed and said, "But she's not going to surgery, and you will stop the event immediately?" "Yes, then I will have Sara and Karen push her to an ambulance entrance, and I will load her into my truck." Jim coughed and said, "Then it's the Eagle's problem?" John nodded. "And when other agencies start looking for the girl?" Jim asked. "She got away." Jim let out a laugh of derision, "Oh yeah, a kid just had her foot blown apart and cut off, and she got up and walked away." John said, "Just work with the girls. I'm going to give Sara the signal, then I have only a matter of minutes to get my truck, the girl, and head for the lair." "And what about me? What do you want me to do?" "I want you to bug out with Chris and come to the lair."

"Chris doesn't know who the Eagle is. Is this how he's gonna find out? And what if he freaks and goes to the cops?" "He will be fine. It will fill in a lot of blanks, and I have a feeling the Eagle is going to need you both to stop this plot." Jim took the cigarette from the back of his ear and stuck it in his mouth and said, "Why is it that the hair on the back of my neck is standing on end? You're going to do it again. I'm not going to get to retire. I swear to God you are going to get me killed." Both men knew that Jim was only being calm because if he lost it in present company he would out everything he knew.

He nodded, and John walked back to the ER, looked at Sara and nodded slowly then vanished. Sara marked the time on the oversized clock in the ER room and then looked over at Karen who had gotten next to her and said, "In thirty seconds, you're going to crash the kid's vitals, and we are going to wheel her out for the OR." Karen said, "She's not going to the OR, is she?" "No. She is headed to meet with the Iron Eagle." Karen smiled as she pulled out a syringe and pulled down a vial of medication. Sara looked over at the clock and whispered, "Now." Karen injected a small amount of liquid into Debbie's IV, and she went into cardiac arrest. The alarms and bells on the monitoring equipment were going off, and Sara called a code blue and yelled, "Karen, get the end of the gurney. We have to get her to an OR, stat." Karen started to push Debbie out the double doors of the ER room, and several doctors started to follow. Jim stepped in front of them and said, "I'm sure Dr. Swenson and Dr. Faber can deal with this. You are all witnesses, and I need you here with my deputies until you have been debriefed."

Sara and Karen were long out of sight and, though there was anger from the doctors and nurses in the room, the cops trumped them.

The black Silverado was parked near an ambulance entrance. Sara gave Debbie a second injection, and her vitals stabilized. They transferred her to a wheelchair and then out the entrance and into the truck. In all the commotion, they were able to load Debbie, and in a flash, the Silverado was on its way to Malibu. Chris and Jim were standing in the ER, and Sara called Jim over and handed him a small satchel. Jim looked at her and whispered, "What's this?" "Just give it to the Eagle. He will know what to do with it."

Jim barked out some other instructions to his team, and he and Chris left. Jim saw Karen and Sara in the hall near the ambulance entrance and asked, "What of the girl?" Sara smiled, "She is in room 3008, or at least that's what the hospital log will show." Jim looked around and said, "You better wipe the surveillance cameras clean, Sara. One of them had to have picked you two up putting the kid in with John." "John told me he would take care of it." Jim smiled and said, "I bet he did. I fuckin' bet he did!" He turned to Chris and said, "Okay, temporary FBI man... you're with me." Chris looked at his watch. It was five p.m. "Where are we going?" Jim laughed as they walked out to his cruiser and said, "Oh...it's a surprise. A really big mother fuckin' surprise."

The music was playing as students and teachers began to arrive at the Anchor Store at the Northridge Mall. Homecoming banners and well decorated windows and walls glistened in silver and blue streamers and white and blue balloons. There were several huge banners that read, "Welcome to Homecoming, Regents," as two bands played on each level of the converted store. Terry Folder and Cathy Hines were working the entrance tables. LAPD school police had set up several metal detectors at all of the entrances and had cleared the building. Students were beginning to file in, but it would be several hours until all of the students would arrive and LAPD worked the detectors to make sure that no one had any weapons.

Several mannequins were littering the exits of the store and had been moved by police when they did their sweep an hour earlier. Jerry Pinskey was hiding in a small dumpster off the main delivery exit watching the police do exactly as he had planned for them to do. He laughed as one of the units was moved over near a pile of clothing and other debris and whispered to himself, "What a bunch of fuckin' rubes. Those bombs are going to set this place ablaze as I fire down on the crowd of cowards." He watched and waited, in no rush. Anyone who could stop him was dead, and no one knew his plot. He started to pull off a pair of coveralls he had on to reveal nice street clothes. He opened the container and stepped out, leaving the coveralls behind and said, "Well, I must join the party. I wouldn't want to miss anything."

CHAPTER EIGHTEEN

"John Swenson goes in...
the Iron Eagle comes out."

The sea was unusually rough for September. A tropical storm moving up from Baja had turned the sea angry. While it was sunny and warm on the coast, off in the distance out over the Pacific there were dark clouds and a gentle wind blowing on shore. John stood in the foyer of the lair, looking out over the wild waves and listening to the sound of the crashing surf and said to himself, "It all seems so appropriate. This strange weather and angry sea in the face of disaster." Jim's voice rose from behind him and said, "It does seem appropriate for the evening, doesn't it?" John didn't turn he just said yes and walked over to the bar and got a bottle of water. Jim walked over and put the satchel down on the granite counter and said, "I was instructed to give these to you." John nodded and walked back over and sat down on one of the couches. "Where's Chris?" John asked. "I dropped him at the main entrance to the house and told him to wait in the living room, that you would come for him."

"So you came in through the tunnel?" Jim nodded and got up and walked over to the bar and poured himself a glass of scotch then walked over to one of the chairs that looked out at the sea and asked, "Where's the girl?" "Sleeping." "Does the Eagle have any other guests?" John nodded. "Coach Trent Hameln from Rosedo High School." "And what the fuck did he do?" John took a drink of his water and said, "Aided and allowed the rape and brutality of young boys." Jim sipped his scotch and asked, "Does that warrant a visit with the Eagle?" John nodded and said, "He also abused young girls at the school for decades. Hameln and Dell had a deal. Hameln agreed to keep Dell's homosexuality and sex with young male students a secret so long as Dell kept watch while Hameln molested and eventually raped and sodomized the girls." "Huh…convenient deal…how many girls?" "Hundreds…no one ever came forward out of fear from what I got out of Dell. I have the confession from Dell on tape."

"The Eagle hasn't tortured a confession out of Hameln yet?" Jim asked, sipping his scotch. "There's been no time. I picked him up near his home early this morning. He also knows about the plot to kill other students that these kids have been hatching." "Really… well that's fuckin' interesting. Did you get that from Dell?" "No. The Rubio kid before he died." "So you tortured and killed the kid?" "No…the kid died as the result of a rape and sodomy overseen by none other than Dell and Hameln. The kid died from sex with Dell because his internal wounds weren't properly healed."

Jim stood up drinking down the last of his scotch and said, "How did the kid die from anal sex?" John said, "He had a bleed, a hemorrhage that the Eagle didn't see until the last few minutes of his life." Jim shook his head and said, "Well, it's six p.m. What do you want to do?" John finished off his bottle of water and said, "Change clothes. You go get Chris. We need to get to these two prisoners fast or else." Jim nodded as John disappeared down the hall in the direction of the holding and operating rooms. Jim watched and said, "John Swenson goes in…the Iron Eagle comes out."

Jim pushed open the secret door into the living room where Chris was sitting on the couch, staring blankly at the sea. Jim coughed a little to alert him of his presence and said, "Your presence is requested in here." Chris stood up and asked, "Where does that door lead?" Jim looked on at him and said, "That's really up to you, man. It could be heaven or hell. For the majority of people who pass this way… it's fuckin' HELL!" Jim pointed to the open door, and Chris walked through and into the foyer of the Eagle's lair.

Trent was awake and alert when the Eagle entered the operating room. Dell's body had gone from rigor mortis to flaccid; his arms hung at his sides, and the white of his remaining eye was now pale gray. Trent screamed at the sight of the Eagle who didn't react. "Tell me what you know about the school rampage plot," the Eagle asked. "What plot…I don't know what you're talking about? Who the hell are you, where am I, and what the hell are you doing with me like this?" Trent was nude and restrained, spread eagle on an operating table. "Oh, Mr. Hameln, I don't have time for games and neither do the children and faculty from your school. I know your secrets. I know what you did to hundreds of young girls at the school you work at."

"I don't know who you think you are, and I don't know what you think you know, but you better explain yourself." The Eagle reared back and struck him right in the groin. The Eagle looked down at the grimacing unable to breathe face of Trent and said, "I don't have time for this, Mr. Hameln. Tell me about the plot to kill students at the school." Trent remained tight-lipped, and the Eagle grabbed a scalpel off a steel tray next to the gurney and drove the blade up under Hameln's scrotum and pulled up on it, splitting his scrotum skin between his two testicles. Hameln screamed and blood began to pool on the gurney between his legs. The Eagle left the scalpel inside him and picked up a remote and turned on the cameras. Trent looked around wildly, seeing his nude body on the screens and the blood pooling between his legs. The Eagle grabbed a clear vial with a white powder in it and shook some of the contents into his palm and rubbed it on Hameln's mouth and lips. Trent started to scream as the compound began to smoke on his face.

"Lye, Mr. Hameln, that's what I put on your mouth. Lye, a bitterly painful and burning chemical." Trent was screaming obscenities as the Eagle poured the solution into Trent's open wound. The scream that Trent let out as the lye hit his scrotum was so loud Jim and Chris heard it in the foyer. Chris stood up and asked, "What the fuck was that?" Jim was sipping his second glass of scotch and said, "Nothing… nothing that you won't get used to hearing." "What the hell is going on here, Jim? That sounded like hell." Jim laughed as he lit a cigarette and said, "You are not far off, kid." The sun was setting, and Chris looked at Jim's profile in the setting sun. The smoke billowing out of his nose and mouth made him look evil, and Chris told him so. Jim laughed, taking a big hit off the smoke and then a drink of his scotch and said, "Hmm…evil. What embodies evil for you, Agent Mantel? What is it that keeps you awake at night? What demons forbid sleep from coming upon you on those sleepless nights? Evil. I look fuckin' evil to you? You haven't seen the face of evil. I used to think that I had seen all of the faces of evil, but I was wrong. Evil comes in all kinds of packages, Mantel, not all of them bad…but when evil that's good comes calling…hell comes with it."

Chris sat with a bottle of water looking at the boiling ocean as lightning flashed out in the distance. There was another scream from the darkness, and Chris asked Jim, "Am I in mortal danger?" Jim took a drink of his scotch and said, "We are all…always in mortal danger, son. Some are just closer to it than others at any given moment." There was another scream resonating out of the darkened hall into the dark foyer, and Jim was looking at Chris. The cherry tip of his cigarette was the only light until a flash of lightning lit up the room, and in that instant Chris looked into Jim's calm, cold eyes, and Jim looked into Chris's eyes of fear. He smiled and said, "Sit down, kid. He will come to you when he's ready for you. You might as well take a breath and relax. The Eagle assists death, which comes for us all sooner or later."

Chris looked down into the black hallway but said nothing. He just sat down in a chair across from Jim in the darkness, the smell of scotch and cigarette smoke heavy in the air, and waited for whoever had called him to this place and for what purpose.

The ping of a ball peen hammer resonated off a small anvil that the Eagle had placed between Hameln's legs. The Eagle said to him as he pushed a shot of adrenaline and another stimulant into Hameln's IV, "Crushed one. Are you going to tell me what you know of the plot, or do you want to taste your left testicle?" Hameln was crying as the Eagle raised the hammer again, and as he did, Hameln screamed, "Homecoming…homecoming…the fuckin' faggot kid Rubio was in a fight with some of my players, and he told one of them that he was going to kill us all, and that there is a plan to kill everyone in the school at homecoming." "Where's that player now?" the Eagle asked in a calm voice. "Dead…he's dead and cremated for all I know. He told it to Brian Donaldson and some others a few days before Brian was murdered."

The Eagle asked, "And Donaldson told you?" Hameln nodded his head weakly, sweat was dripping down his face, and his eyes were full of tears." The Eagle asked, "And you did nothing?" Hameln spit on the ground and said, "You don't deal with high school kids, do you? They talk shit all the time. They make threats. It's all part of the game. I wasn't about to make an issue of something some little faggot told one of my players in the heat of a fight." The Eagle was still holding the small hammer in the air over Trent's one good nut and asked, "When is homecoming?" Hameln was catching his breath and said, "Um…what day is it?" "Sunday. The first Sunday of September.

"It's tonight…homecoming is tonight." "At the school?" "No…at an Anchor Store that was closed down at Northridge Mall. The mall donated the store to the school for the dance and homecoming party, so the faculty and school police could oversee the students better. Rosedo has a huge gang problem, so it is a more controlled environment. There's no way they can do anything. The LAPD school division will have metal detectors and all kinds of security. There's no way that Rubio or anyone else is going to bust in with guns blazing."

The Eagle raised the hammer and brought it crashing down on Hameln's other testicle, and it popped like a grape, sending blood and flesh onto the Eagle's plastic face mask. Hameln let out a hard scream and then blacked out. The Eagle twisted the scalpel that was still inserted into the sack, and with a flick of the wrist emasculated Hameln. Arterial spray was pouring out of the open wound. The Eagle didn't bother to stop it. He allowed Hameln to bleed out on the table then wheeled all of the corpses to the incinerator and threw them in one after the other. He threw in their personal belongings as well and pushed the start button, and the unit came to life, ridding the world of more scum. He turned his attention to operating room two and Debbie Atwater.

Jade Morgan had positively identified the remains of Tim Elliott as well as Alan Marks who she had picked up from the hospital earlier after Marks had decided on a suicide shootout with John and Chris. She had her orderly put the bodies in the cooler and was going to notify the next of kin when Jessica Holmes walked into her office. She sat down with a couple of backpacks and some pieces of paper and said, "These things were with the bodies." She handed the pieces of paper to Jade who looked them over and said, "They look like usernames and passwords for some website but not one that I've ever heard of." Jessica opened the two backpacks and said, "There are two laptops here. Why didn't law enforcement take these?" "Who the fuck knows, Jessica? I've stopped asking myself those questions. I spend half my time doing police work and the other half as a medical examiner."

Jade took the two laptop cases and noticed that they both had two blinking lights on the side of them; one was red and the other blue. Jessica looked at the lights well and watched as Jade slowly began to slide the lock on the first laptop to open it. Jessica yelled, "STOP!" The scream startled Jade who almost dropped the computer on the floor. "What the fuck, Jessica?" "Don't open the laptops." "Why the fuck not?" Jade was pissed, and Jessica looked at them closely and said, "What do you know about these victims?" Jade was frustrated and said, "Nothing, Jessica, not a goddamn thing. What does it matter? There might be next of kin information on this Alan Marks kid." Jessica looked at Jade and said, "Call John…I don't think these are regular laptops. I think they are more than that, something a lot more dangerous." Jade looked at her like she had three heads and said, "What the fuck? Is your fuckin' minor in criminology?" "Yeah…that's one of the prerequisites to get into your line of work." Jade just shook her head and called John.

Chris and Jim were sitting silently in the foyer. Screams of pain and anguish had been emanating from the dark corridor for quite a while. Chris took a breath and was about to speak when he saw a figure appear in the hall and start walking toward them. "Have you seen enough to know that there is major trouble brewing, Agent Mantel?" The voice was unfamiliar, and the figure towered over him and Jim. Chris looked to Jim for reaction, but all Jim did was light another cigarette and take a sip of his scotch before saying, "Answer the Iron Eagle's question, Chris." Chris stood up grabbing for his weapon, but the Eagle disarmed him and pushed him back down into the chair.

"This is no time for games. Have you learned anything from the lessons of the past several days?" "Yes, I have. What have you done with John Swenson?" Jim let out a little laugh, and the Eagle said, "Swenson is just fine. I have learned of a plot to kill hundreds of students of a local high school at their homecoming dance tonight at an Anchor Store in the Northridge Mall." Chris perked up and asked, "That's what the screaming was all about. You were torturing some poor bastard for information." "I was definitely torturing someone, but he was by no means an innocent man. Jim, I need you and Agent Mantel to go to the mall and get into the store." Jim looked up at the Eagle and asked, "And do what? You want a SWAT team in the place? Do you want me to order an evacuation?" "No…I want you and Agent Mantel to blend in with the others. Wear street clothes. Take positions on the upper level of the store out of sight of the students, faculty, and police."

"What…like sniper positions?" "Observational positions with the ability to shoot in every direction." "How many shooters are we dealing with?" "I don't know for certain. I'm going to get that information next. I think a single, but a very, very heavily armed and well-trained shooter. There are most likely booby traps on all of the exits to the store with an emphasis on maximum kill for those who try to flee when the shooting starts." "Then I need to order in SWAT and the bomb squad." The Eagle was steady and intent in his tone, "Jim, if you send in a SWAT team and bomb squad all that you will get out of it are a lot of full body bags. The guy will blow up the store, killing as many as he can and move on to plan B if he has one, and given what I know of the killer, he has one."

Jim stood up and walked over to the wet bar and washed out his glass and put it on the counter. "Let's go, Chris. You're already in street clothes. I need to stop by my house to change and to get some high powered weapons." Chris stood up, and the Eagle said, "Jim, you can take what you need from my armory. You know where to go and have access. The weapons and ammunition are untraceable." Jim nodded, and Chris said, "Wait…Sheriff, you know who the Iron Eagle is?" "Yeah…what about it?" "You're taking direction from a cold-blooded killer? Have you forgotten that we are lawmen? You're a lawman. You don't take directions; you take him into custody." Both Jim and the Eagle laughed, and Jim said, "You don't know what I know about this man…the Iron Eagle…if he gives me instructions, I have learned over several years to listen."

Jim looked over at the Eagle and said, "That didn't always keep me from getting FUCKIN' SHOT! But I listen. He knows what he's talking about, and no one who has ended up in the talons of the Eagle was innocent. They deserved everything they got and some deserved to die even worse. Now, let's go. I have a feeling we don't have much time." Chris turned back to say something to the Eagle, but he was gone, and Jim and Chris were suddenly standing alone in the foyer. The lights had come on, and Jim was walking back into the dark hallway where the screams and pleas had come from. He was waving his arm with a cigarette in his hand and saying, "Let's go, kid. We don't have a lot of time."

John was sitting in the conference room of his lair looking at Deborah Atwater, asleep on a gurney, on the TV monitor. His cell phone rang, and he answered, "Swenson." "John, it's Jade. I have two laptop computers from two victims, Tim Elliott and the kid you wasted at the hospital. I also have documents that came from their belongings which have user names and passwords for a web address I have never heard of." John asked, "Can you use your computer in the office to video chat with me?" "Yeah, hang on." John took his phone and plugged it into a single cable that spread in several different directions in the conference room. Jade popped up on one of the large video monitors in the room and asked, "Can you see us?" John could see Jessica and Jade and two closed laptop computers on her desk. "Yes…I can see you both fine. Did you open the laptops?" Jessica shouted out, "No John…I think they are more than laptops. I think they might be bombs." "Bring the camera around to each laptop and show me what you're worried about, Jessica."

Jessica picked up the camera and walked over to each laptop and filmed them as John looked on. John said, "Jade, don't open the laptops. Jessica is right. They are booby-trapped. Can you bring them to me here at the house?" "Um…yeah. I suppose. What's on them and how are you going to deal with them?" "That's my problem, just bring them here. They will remain stable so long as you don't open them. They have lock latches on the front of them. Don't touch anything, just get them here as soon as possible." John hung up then pulled out the Iron Eagle's mask. "It's time to have a chat with Ms. Atwater."

CHAPTER NINETEEN

"I've seen you. I've heard you,
and I will be watching you!"

It was half past eight p.m. when Billy Stone and several of his friends walked through the doors at the Anchor Store and to the table to get their badges. Billy stood staring at Cathy Hines and Mary Rubin and said, "Well, bitches, are you going to give me and my friends our goddamn name tags, or are you going to stand there staring at us?" Mary pushed the sign-in book to Billy who picked it up and threw it back at her. "I'm not signing your goddamn book. You and your pals here are a bunch of fuckin' nerds." An LAPD officer saw and heard Billy and approached, "Mr. Stone, you apologize to these young ladies." "Fuck you, fake cop man. You're lucky I don't kick your ass." The officer grabbed Billy by the hair and pulled him to the side away from the other guests. At five foot three and eighty pounds, Stone was no match for the force of the cop.

"Now you listen to me, you little shit, I'll beat you and put your ass in a dumpster outside of this building. You will be respectful, and you will apologize, or you will deal with the service end of my nightstick.

You got it?" Stone skulked back to the table, his pale white skin and pimpled face, red with embarrassment. His short black hair, which was his pride and joy, was messed up, and he snorted out a derisive, "Sorry," and took the tags and handed them to the other three that were with him. The cop looked at Billy and his followers and said, "I've seen you. I've heard you, and I will be watching you!" Stone walked off in the direction of a buffet in search of more trouble. What Billy didn't know was that the LAPD was not the only person who saw him come into the party…Jerry Pinskey was standing on the upper landing, looking over the railing near one of the four dance floors in the store and saw him come in. He had seen the whole altercation and had a grin from ear to ear as he watched Billy set off for the buffet.

He spoke under his breath to himself, "Now that the final individual victim has arrived…let the killing begin." He walked through the crowded dance floor and off into a dark corner of the upper level.

Jade and Jessica walked into John's house at just after eight. They entered the living room and called out, but there was no immediate reply. Jade poured herself a drink and asked Jessica if she wanted anything. "Coke Zero, please. I know that John keeps plenty of those for himself." Jade threw Jessica a bottle of soda, and she said, "Thanks a fuckin' lot, Jade. Now I have to let it settle or get another." Jessica was shaking her head as she walked over and pulled another from the fridge and opened it. Jade was about to say something else when the front door opened, and Sara and Karen walked in. Jade laughed and said, "Well, look who the cat dragged in."

Sara shot her a dirty look, and Karen said, "Not now, Jade. Not after the damn day we have had." Jade and Jessica laughed, and Jade said, "Somehow, I don't think that this day is anywhere near over." Sara looked around and asked, "Where's John?" "Beats the fuck out of me. I called him because we found two laptops that the two dead kids had on them, and he said to bring them over right away." Sara stood looking at the two backpacks and said, "Two dead kids? You only took one body." "Yes…well, there was a murder in Northridge, and I had scooped up that body before the hospital event took place. I figured the laptops might give me information on the next of kin on the guys, and John wanted the computers here." Sara took a glass and filled it with ice and poured herself a scotch while handing Karen another Coke Zero. Karen sat down next to Jessica who started to say, "I wouldn't do that," as she cracked open the bottle only to have it explode all over her and Jessica. She continued her statement slowly, covered in the soft drink, "if I were you."

Jade looked on and said, "Oops, sorry…I threw that to Jessica a few minutes ago." Sara shook her head and threw Karen a towel. She was drying off and heading to the sink near the wet bar saying, "How the fuck could this day get any worse?"

"It's going to get a lot worse if I don't see those laptops and get information out of Atwater," John said. Jade pointed to the backpacks on the floor and said, "Here they are, and here are the papers Jessica found among the victims' belongings." John took the documents, looked at them, and then grabbed the backpacks and asked Jade to follow him. The others sat and spoke quietly as John and Jade disappeared into the Eagle's lair.

Rosedo's homecoming dance was really rolling. The floors were full of boys and girls of all ages. Students and teachers danced under disco lights. Two DJs were calling out for requests and spinning vinyl albums and making rap music sounds. The tables on the lower level near the buffet were full of gabbing preteen and teenage boys and girls whose biggest concern was who liked who, who hated who, and if what they were wearing was cool or not. Most of them had some type of electronic device in their hands, and they were taking self photographs or shots with their friends and uploading them to their favorite social media sites. The only event bigger than homecoming for these students was the prom. Sure, for the seniors, graduation was the end all be all, but the seniors were the minority, and they had broken off from the rest of the group and formed their own corner of the store. While there was no official separation of events, the underclassman allowed the seniors to commandeer a dance floor on the lower level as well as several large areas of the store for themselves. There was plenty of room, and for a school known for its racial and gang violence, the party was a nice respite from the day-to-day violence and disruptions they dealt with. The fact that there was a strong police and faculty presence hadn't hurt the event either, so things was fun and calm.

Billy Stone was tormenting a pair of freshmen near a back restroom. They were taunting two boys that were trying to have a good time. He had lured them away with the promise of some weed and now had them in a dark corner out of sight of police and others. Randy Gilchrist was taking the brunt of the abuse. He was a nerdy ninth grader known for his great intelligence and passive nature. Billy had him pinned to the floor and was smacking him in the face. "What? Come on…don't whine, talk…what's that you say…you little pussy… you too fuckin' smart to talk to us?" Randy was crying and trying to speak, but Billy was sitting on his chest, making getting a breath difficult. Billy looked at the freshman pinned against the walls by his buddies. They were taking turns punching the kid in the stomach.

He said, "Hey…guys…let's take them into the bathroom and really fuck them up." He winked at one of his friends, who grabbed Randy and drug him inside. Billy was the last to get in there and grabbed Randy by the hair and threw him down on the white tile floor and said, "All right you two, strip off your clothes." The boys refused, and Billy and his crew pulled out razor knives and box cutters. Billy slashed Randy across the arm with the blade and said, "Strip, you mother fuckers, or we'll hack you to pieces." One of the guys with Billy said, "Smart move, taping the plastic cutters to our legs under our socks, so they didn't get picked up by the metal detectors." Billy laughed as he removed another from his other leg and said, "Yeah, and they call this piece of shit a genius." He was pointing to Randy, who was standing with the other boy in his underwear.

"I said strip…mother fuckers…underwear, too…get them off and pile your clothes right in front of me." The boys did as instructed and now stood nude against the bathroom wall. Billy ordered their clothes picked up and thrown in the trash outside the bathroom. The naked boys looked on as Billy unzipped his fly and pulled out his penis.

Sara and Karen joined John and Jade in the Eagle's lair. Sara looked at him and said, "Here is the drug." Jade took the syringe out of Sara's hand and the five stood looking at Debbie Atwater who was asleep when Jade gave her the injection of SP-117; the drug worked almost instantly, and Debbie was alert and talkative. "Where are Alan, Tim, Mark, and Jerry?" The Eagle sat next to her on the gurney and said, "All but you and Jerry Pinskey are dead." Debbie began to scream, and Sara slapped her on the side of her face and said, "Silence! We need answers, not your whiny ass shit." The Eagle said, "You killed several young girls two nights ago." Debbie fell silent and asked, "How could you know that?" The Eagle stared into Debbie's eyes with his own dead black icy stare through his mask and said, "It's my job to know these things. I know that you have helped with several killings, and that you are in on the killings for homecoming." Debbie started to cry and said, "Oh God…you're going to kill me."

Sara reached down and pulled the bandage off Debbie's lower leg where her foot had been amputated and handed the bandages to Karen who laid them on a steel hospital tray next to the gurney. Sara said, "All I have to do is remove two stitches, and you will bleed to death right here, right now. Do I want to kill you? Yes…I do. I think you deserve it, but that's not my call. It's up to the Iron Eagle if you live or die, so answer his questions and do it now." Sara was dressed in a white hospital coat with a surgical hat and mask on and a plastic face mask as were the other women in the room. Debbie asked, "What do you want to know?" The Eagle had Tim Elliott's laptop open and the TOR screen up. There was an instant message window in a chat room open as well, and he asked, "I have read all of the plans of Mr. Elliott as well as Alan Marks. I have read their manifesto and what they plan to do, the killings that they planned, and are planning. I have also read the manifesto of Jerry Pinskey."

Debbie screamed, "Jerry has lost his mind. He's going to try to do it all alone." "Explain!" The Eagle had every monitor on in the room, recording everything that Debbie was saying. It was ten after nine when Debbie finished talking, and she had given the Eagle all he needed to deal with Pinskey. The Eagle looked down at the half-naked girl and said, "I was out at Valley Circle. I heard what Johnny Belk and his friends had done to those boys. I know they couldn't go to the school or the police, and I don't blame them for the actions they chose to take. All of their attackers are dead except Bill Stone." Debbie yelled out, "He's the worst of all of them. He's a sick twisted fuck who takes pleasure in raping and torturing anything with two legs."

"I know." "And what are you going to do about it, Mr. Eagle? What are you going to do to stop this massacre? They are all there. If Jerry has set the bombs, then he will start to shoot every person in that store, and there's nothing you can do to stop him." The Eagle sat back and looked at the clock on the wall; it was a quarter past nine. "I have forty-five minutes before he is to start shooting, according to you," the Eagle said. Debbie responded, "Unless he kills Billy first. If he kills Billy, and he's alone, he will most likely start killing everyone ASAP and exact his revenge and then bug out before anyone knows what happened."

The Eagle stood up and told Sara, "I have to get to the mall. Can you handle things here?" Sara nodded, and Karen said, "We have things covered here. Do what you need to do." Debbie said, "I know your voice, lady…you're that doctor at the ER who was trying to save me and my foot. You were the one who talked Alan down until the FBI came in the room and killed him. You're doctor…Faber…yeah. The kid doctor. As soon as I'm well, I'm going to the media, and I'm going to tell them all about you. They might lock me up…but I will take all of you with me."

The Eagle turned around and said, "No…Debbie…no, you won't. You killed and assisted in the killing of several people. You're not going to prison or jail." Debbie let out a loud laugh and said, "I knew I would get away with it…I have you fuckers by the balls. I hate that Alan, Timmy, and Mark are dead…but then as Jerry always says, 'shit happens.' Jerry and I were keeping our relationship a secret until after the rampage for homecoming. He planned to shoot the others during the attacks, and he and I would run off and be together in Aruba. No one knows about that but us. He had to work so hard to hold back his love for me. Shit, he even blew part of my foot off as I ran with Alan…I couldn't let him get away…Alan would have gone to the cops. He so loved me, and he thought I loved him…HA! Joke's on his dead ass. I love only Jerry, and as soon as he has finished the killing we will be together."

The Eagle said, "Yes…Debbie…the one thing I can promise you is that as soon as I'm finished with Jerry Pinskey you two will be together in whatever world lies beyond this one." Sara had a syringe full of a light blue liquid in her hand, and the Eagle said to Debbie as he took the syringe from Sara and stuck the needle into the IV in her arm, "This is really, really going to hurt. You might have killed your victims with a quick shot to the head, but you're not going to be so lucky." The Eagle injected the fluid into the IV, and Debbie began to scream almost instantly. He said, "I'm sorry it could not have worked out differently, but I will make sure if I can that Jerry sees your dead body." And with that, the Eagle left the room headed for the mall.

The women stood watching Debbie as her veins started to turn black as the liquid began to race for her heart to be pushed through her body. Debbie screamed at Sara, "You're a doctor. You're supposed to save lives. Stop this…oh God, it hurts. Stop this, you bitch." Sara walked over to the table and said, "No can do, kid." She injected a clear follow up liquid into the IV and said, "Have a nice death…I have to get some dinner. I'm starving as are my guests." The women went to walk away as the drug hit Debbie's heart and started to rush through her body. Sara looked at the screaming girl writhing in agony and said, "Oh…I almost forgot…MAY GOD NOT HAVE MERCY ON YOUR SOUL!" Sara shut off the lights and closed the operating room door as Debbie screamed into the cold darkness and into the abyss of her own agony. Sara whispered to herself as she walked with the others, "It will take a couple of hours for you to die, kid; you might still have some breath in you if the Eagle decides to bring your lover back."

She closed off the secret passage to the lair and asked the others, "So, who's hungry?" All hands went up. "Well then, Jade give Barb a call and see if she would like to join us for a little girls night out at Santiago's." Jade called her while Sara walked on to the bedroom to shower and change.

CHAPTER TWENTY

"Holy shit...I'm dead!"

Jim and Chris arrived at the mall at nine p.m. They walked in and showed their IDs, and one of the LAPD officers asked, "Do you have someone here at this gathering, Sheriff? A grandkid or something?" Jim laughed and said, "Yeah…something like that. Stay on your toes. I hear these high school parties can get pretty crazy." The cop laughed as Chris and Jim disappeared into the crowd.

The music was loud, and the screams and laughter of young boys and girls was deafening. Chris leaned in and asked, "What are we to do? Where do you want to stage?" Jim pointed to opposite sides of the upper level of the store turned nightclub and said, "Get up there. We will be across from each other. Keep your eyes peeled. You have this Pinskey guy's photograph?" "Yeah, but I don't need it. I have it burned into my memory." Jim grabbed Chris's collar and pulled him close and whispered, "They all look alike at this age, Chris. Don't be so fuckin' arrogant as to think that you could spot that kid so easily in this crowd. You have fucked up a lot in the past two days. You end up killing an innocent kid, and I will shoot you myself, and that's not a threat. It's a fuckin' promise." Chris pulled away but could see from the look on Jim's face he wasn't kidding. Chris removed the photo of Pinskey from his pocket and took a good hard look at it. Jim smiled, pointed, and walked away.

The black Silverado pulled up at the back of the store. There was no outside security in the parking lot because all of the action was inside the mall. The Eagle pulled one duffle bag from the back of his truck along with some extra body armor plates that he put onto his chest, abdomen, and legs. There were several emergency entrances onto the roof of the mall and its stores that only police and fire knew about. He pressed one of the small remotes on his belt clip, and the ladder lowered, allowing roof access to the Anchor Store where the homecoming party was going on. He put the bag in his mouth and climbed to the rooftop then made his way across until he got to the entrance. The roof access lock was electromagnetic with a manual override keyed entry for fire or police in case they didn't have a remote unit to unlock the doors. The Eagle pressed the button on the side of a remote scanner on his belt, and in seconds, the lock clicked open. He pulled open the roof access, and the sound of loud music and laughter escaped, letting him know he was in the right place.

The Eagle held the bag in his mouth as he descended the ladder into the attic of the store. He pressed the night vision on his mask and quickly located an entrance. He pulled six electronic remote detonator blockers from the bag and then turned on a signal transfer detector seeking out the distinct ping that a remote detonator would put off. The unit was going crazy in his hand as it scanned frequency after frequency. There was so much chatter being picked up by the unit because of all the cell phone and electronic activity in the store below. The unit's green screens streamed with pulses like a cardiac monitor on a heart patient, and he watched the readings until the green line went flat with one lone pulse tone, and, in that moment, the Eagle knew he had found the remote detonator signals, and much to his surprise, it was a singular pulse, which meant they were all on a single frequency. He plugged a remote detonator block into the scanner. The two units took several seconds syncing until the remote tone on the green screen had no reading, and the lights on the remote went from red to green.

The Eagle sighed in relief and said to himself, "There, now all of the remote detonators are blocked and disabled. That won't save anyone who tries to exit the store where this guy might have put standard booby traps, though." The Eagle was talking to himself as he pulled up the blueprints to the store and all of its possible exits. His tablet was the only light in the attic, and the music droned on as he looked for access to all exits that could kill potential victims.

Several girls were dancing and laughing only a few feet from where Jim had set himself up to look for Pinskey. He stared down over the railing and around the upper level of the store looking for his target. There were blind spots where he couldn't see, and he mumbled to himself, "Those dark fuckers are the problem because that's where that fucker is, hiding in a shadowy hallway, waiting for his moment to attack."

Chris was on one of three escalators in the store, heading to the upper level when he saw Pinskey out of the corner of his eye. He looked hard at the figure standing in the shadow of the lower level and checked the photograph again when he reached the top and was certain he had found his man. He turned around and started down the escalator for the lower level, looking over into the shadowy corner. Pinskey was standing still, too still. Chris got to the floor and started to walk in his direction while trying to keep a low profile, but at six foot six and two hundred and eighty pounds of pure muscle, he was as inconspicuous as a black dot on a white canvas. Students who were dancing and frolicking stopped in his presence and stepped out of his way.

Chatter started all around him, and he could hear the kids talking in clipped and hushed tones, "Who the fuck is he?" "My God…look at him. He's a fuckin' stud. Is he a new teacher?" The chatter went on then died down, and the kids went back to their dancing and talking. He got to the corner where he had seen Jerry, but he was gone when he got there. Chris walked into the darkness, which to his surprise led into another well lit area that held janitorial closets as well as bathrooms and storage areas for store products.

He walked the perimeter of the area, looking for Jerry, but there was no sign of him. He pushed the swinging doors that led into the storage area of the lower level, and, to his surprise, they opened freely. He walked into the dimly lit area and saw several weapons near the far back wall. He pulled his service revolver and came to a stash of M-16 rifles. He saw two of the units as well as dozens of extra capacity clips for the guns. He grabbed three clips of ammunition as well as the rifle and made his way back to the swinging doors. Just as he entered the empty hall, he heard the sound of male voices echoing off the walls of a room nearby and moved slowly, following the sound.

Jerry Pinskey had heard the same commotion that Chris did only they were on opposite sides of the noise. He recognized Billy's voice clearly resonating off the walls of the men's room. "I didn't fuckin' stutter. Get on your knees and lick your shit off of my cock!" Jerry pulled a Taurus nine millimeter from his jacket pocket. The gun was small and easily concealed. It had also been modified by Tim and machined and tapped for a screw-on silencer, which fit in his pocket as one silent weapon. Jerry pulled back on the stock to load the gun; the extra capacity clip allowed the gun to hold double the bullets it would usually carry. He had an extra clip in the side pocket of his pants, which he felt for to make sure it was there. He pushed the door open to peek in and saw two boys, one was bent over a toilet while an older boy he didn't recognize sodomized him. The kid was screaming and crying, but his head was pressed down into the bowl. The second boy was on his knees, crying and holding his lower abdomen.

Jerry knew what he had already been through. Billy Stone was standing nude with his cock covered in a dark substance, and Jerry stepped into the room with the gun trained at Billy's head. "It wasn't enough that you and your sick fuck friends did that to me, Alan, Tim, and Mark? You and these new sick fucks are doing it again? You're not getting away with it, Billy. Not this time!" Billy froze.

The Eagle moved into the upper level of the store and dropped into a storage area. The music was loud as were the kids who were partying like there was no tomorrow. He turned off his night vision and moved quietly through the storage room. He found two M-16s and extra capacity clips and quickly disabled the weapons' firing pins and took the clips and put them into his duffle bag. "If there is this much here, he has to have more weapons in other parts of this store."

There was an exit sign at the end of the storage room, and the Eagle moved to it to see that the remote bombs were disabled but that Pinskey had also set up several booby traps with hand grenades with the pins pulled and jammed in between door handles. "A perfect kill. This guy knows what the hell he's doing." The Eagle was able to remove the grenades one by one and disable them. He looked around at the rest of the room and saw no other materials. He moved back to the vent and started through it, headed in the direction of each of the exits and emergency exits to the store to disable the rest.

Jim's radio crackled on his hip, and he pulled it out and said, "This is O'Brian. Over." "There are bombs and booby traps all over this place, Jim…every exit and emergency exit. I just disabled one set and two M-16s." The Eagle's voice crackled over the radio, and he gave Jim a new channel setting to switch to. Jim made the change and raised the Eagle and said, "Fuck…I haven't seen the Pinskey guy, and I have lost sight of Chris…what the fuck do you want me to do?"

There was some static then the Eagle said, "Get to the main level. There are three exits and one emergency exit. If it's only Pinskey, he has a shitload of fire power. You need to make sure not to start a panic. If these kids start running for the exits, it's going to be a blood bath. You need to disable the weapons and stow the clips. If he has stayed true to what I have seen, there will be two remote detonate bombs. Don't worry about them. I disabled them. The guy has three hand grenades in the door handles though. The minute someone hits those doors the grenades will go off, and the explosion from the grenades could set off the remote bombs."

Jim made his way to a service elevator at the back of the upper level. He got in and pressed for the ground floor. He spoke back into the radio and asked, "So, they are fragmentation grenades?" "Yes…three in use, pins pulled, two pressed between the double door handles and one pin out pressed between the split between the two doors for when they open at the top. It's a perfect kill pattern. This guy knows what he's doing." Jim was walking through a dark corridor toward an exit sign and came to a storage room with double swinging doors. "I'm at a far end storage room. Are the doors secure?" The Eagle said yes, so Jim moved in and headed for the exit, spotting the M-16s right away. He disarmed the weapons immediately and stowed the clips in a storage locker. "Okay…I have disabled the guns and stowed the clips. This fucker is planning a blood bath."

The Eagle had dropped down into another storage area and made a beeline for the exits. "Roger that, Jim. I found another set up and am disarming the weapons and stowing the clips." Jim was looking at the booby-trapped door and asked, "What if I move the remotes?" "Negative. I disabled their remote detonation capability. I don't know if there are any other traps outside of the doors. Do you remember how to disarm a fragmentation grenade?" Jim looked at the doors and said, "Well, shit, Mr. fuckin' Eagle, it's only been some forty-five years since I learned it…in the corps." The Eagle came back over the radio and said, "If you can't do it tell me, then you will have to figure out a way to get to Chris and try to keep the calm and kill Pinskey." Jim had already removed two of the grenades and disabled them, and he had pulled the last one from the top of the door, holding the detonator clip closed while disassembling it. Sweat was dripping down his face as he released the final pin and dropped the grenade to the floor.

"Okay…fuck…I cleared this exit. How many have you done?" "I just finished the second one." "How many fuckin' more are there?" "Two more on your level and one left on mine." The Eagle had crawled back into the duct work and was heading for the last exit when Jim said, "I'm moving to the second exit. The final exits are all the ones that are marked with red exit signs, right? Are there any secret exits that this fucker could have done this to?" Jim asked. The Eagle said, "There are several other exits, but they are not known to the general public. I know where they are, and you would know if this were a hostage or other situation, but that's it."

Jim was walking into the storage room and to the emergency exit doors. He found the same gun setup, disabled the weapons and the grenades, and moved on to the final exit. There was radio silence as they worked to try and clear the scene. Jim made his way to the emergency exit, and the Eagle dropped down into the final room and had everything disabled in a matter of minutes. There was a crackle over the radio, and Jim must have had the button on his radio pressed because the Eagle heard him say in a soft voice, "Holy shit…I'm dead!"

CHAPTER TWENTY-ONE

"I just saw my fuckin' life pass before MY FUCKIN' EYES."

You could hear a pin drop in the bathroom on the upper level. Pinskey stood with his gun trained on Billy, and the others were cowering in a corner of the men's room. He pulled out a small gray box and said, "You see this, asshole…when I'm finished killing you, I'm going to kill everyone in the goddamn building. What do you think of that, you fuckin' piece of shit?" Silence and tears met Jerry's revelation. "Down on your knees, assholes." They didn't move, and Pinskey fired the weapon above their heads. There was no sound from the gun just the ricochet of the bullet off the white tile walls and into the leg of one of the guys with Stone who let out a loud yelp.

"Oh, shut the fuck up," Jerry said, pointing the gun at another overweight thug and shooting him in the head. Stone slowly went to his knees as did the others, looking at the blood and brains of their friend dripping down the walls of the toilet stall.

"Oh, Jesus, Jerry, we were just kidding around, man…I'm sorry. What can I do to make it up to you?" Billy was trembling with his hands over his head. "Make it up to me…how the fuck can you make it up to me…you raping and bullying bastard?" Jerry was trembling himself, not with fear, but anger. "Take off your clothes, you prick." Billy shook his head, and Jerry wasted no time putting a bullet into the head of another one of Billy's friends.

Billy screamed. "Now…take off your goddamn clothes. Strip nude or the next one is going between your eyes." Stone started taking off his clothes as the others watched. He was shaking violently as piece by piece his clothing came off, and he stood nude before Jerry. "Now turn around and get into the toilet stall." Billy didn't move fast enough, and Jerry shot all of the people in the room. He ordered Stone to bend over the toilet, and as he did, Pinskey dropped his pants.

Chris heard a yelp coming from the bathroom and moved fast in that direction with his weapon in his hand. He didn't see the three girls coming out of the restroom next door, but they saw him running for the men's room door with a gun in his hand. The girls screamed in unison and ran for the dance floor, crying and screaming, "Gun… gun…there's a man with a gun!"

The Eagle had made it onto the landing near the bathroom, heard the screaming girls, and saw Chris running with his gun drawn. He grabbed his radio and called out to Jim, "Jim…Chris just sent this place into a panic. Where are you?" Silence met his call.

Chris made his way to the bathroom and burst through the doors as the whole store erupted into total panic and kids started running for the exits as police, armed with heavy weapons, descended on the store's entrance.

Chris pushed open the door to the inner men's room and saw Jerry Pinskey sodomizing a boy at gunpoint. "Freeze!" Chris cried, pointing his weapon at Jerry. Chris had his back nearly against the entrance door to the bathroom, and Pinskey turned his body with his cock still up Stone's ass and said, "You're not taking this away from me, cop. You so much as blink, and I will blow his head off." Chris stood frozen with his gun on Pinskey, helpless to stop what he was doing to Stone. Jerry pumped and grunted until his body shuddered in orgasm.

"How did you like that, Billy? Did you like feeling my cock cum then throb and fill your ass, you dirt bag?" Jerry pulled away from Billy with his back to Chris and said, "You don't know it, cop…but you just killed everyone in this place including yourself." Jerry jerked forward and fell to the floor. Chris fired, missing Jerry and striking Billy Stone right in the anus. Billy hit the floor, blood gushing from his wound. Pinskey turned to fire at Chris when a giant dressed in black rammed open the doors, throwing Chris to the floor, knocking him unconscious. The towering figure walked slowly toward Jerry who fired three shots, but the Eagle kept moving as if nothing had happened.

He pulled a weapon from his hip and said, "I hope you feel better," and shot Jerry in the neck with a tranquilizer dart. Pinskey dropped the weapon and pulled a gray box from his jacket pocket. "It's time to kill you all!" He pressed the button on the remote detonator but nothing happened. He slid down the front of a toilet, and the Eagle lifted him to his masked face and said, "Your rampage is over. The kids are safe. Now, you're coming with me." He grabbed Chris and Jerry and opened a large side vent in the wall and threw the two men into it. He pushed the unconscious men until he reached a large opening then stepped over their bodies, kicked open a steel grate that exited the building, and pulled them out and put them in his truck.

The Eagle called out over the radio to Jim, "Jim, Jim…are you out there? I didn't hear an explosion. Are you okay?" There was silence on the radio. "Jim, Jim…I have Pinskey and Chris. I left a calling card of the Eagle along with the evidence against all of the players in this plot and the role they played. Can you get out?" There was another moment of silence, and the Eagle ripped off his mask and was getting ready to run back into the mall when Jim's voice came over the radio. "I just saw my fuckin' life pass before MY FUCKIN' EYES…Jesus fuckin' Christ. I'm okay…I will get the fuck out of here and meet you back at the lair, OUT!"

The Eagle pulled the Silverado out onto Tampa Avenue headed for the 101 Freeway and Malibu. As he drove, ambulances and fire trucks as well as SWAT and LAPD units were rolling past him headed for the mall.

CHAPTER TWENTY-TWO

"'What happened in there?
The Eagle happened in there."

The Northridge Mall was a frantic scene, kids running in all directions. Police had pulled back after there was unidentified material that looked like bombs. The bomb squad had been called in, and students, teachers, and others were gathering in the parking lot as police called out to anyone left in the building to come out with their hands in the air.

Jim was sitting with his back against a wall in one of the storage rooms. He had been able to diffuse the last grenade and was now trying not to get stepped on as kids were running through the very door that only minutes earlier would have been a death trap. He got to his feet and switched his radio back to police frequency and started walking past the stragglers of children pushing their way out. They were running over each other, and Jim yelled loudly and said, "YOU'RE FUCKIN' SAFE…JUST WALK!" He pulled the radio off his belt and called out to LAPD as well as SWAT, announcing he was inside the building and that the building was clear. Jim leaned against an entrance pillar to the store as officers approached with weapons drawn. He held his badge in his left hand high in the air and yelled, "If one of you dumb fucks shoots me by mistake and I survive, I will kill you!" Riggs was leading the way into the store and got to Jim and asked, "Shit, Jim, are you okay?" "Do I look like I'm mother fuckin' okay? Shit, man. I've been in a war zone." Riggs helped Jim to a bench just outside the store as the commotion went on around them.

"What the fuck happened in there?" Riggs asked. Jim took a cigarette out of his top left pocket and pulled his Zippo out, lit up, and said, "What happened in there? The Eagle happened in there." Riggs had a confused look on his face. "The Eagle was trying to kill a bunch of kids?" Riggs asked. Jim shook his head and said, "No, you dumbass. The Eagle just saved a shitload of kids. There are some bodies in there, but they are just a few of the bad guys and unfortunately their victims. None of the dead were killed by the Eagle. I know that as fact. When the scope of what was planned for tonight is revealed, it will send shivers up your spine." Jim took a deep drag off the cigarette, and Riggs pulled one out himself and lit it and asked, "Is there no end to what the fuckin' Eagle is capable of?"

Jim stood up and walked over to the store entrance, and as he walked with a bit of a limp, he said, "The Eagle is human, Riggs. He's flesh and blood like you and me, and if you ask me, not only is there an end to what he can do, I have a feeling he's getting sick and tired of doing our fuckin' jobs. Yeah Riggs. There's an end to what the Eagle can do, and it scares the hell out of me to think about this city without him, without his constant presence saving lives and meting out justice. There is an end, and I think that end might be closer than any of us might think." Riggs took a hit off the cigarette and put it out on the concrete walk outside the store and followed Jim back inside to process the scene.

Jerry Pinskey was strapped to a gurney next to Debbie Atwater. He looked over to see her glazed eyes and tear-stained face, looking off into some far off place. The Eagle walked in, and he was in street clothes, a pair of blue jeans, a tight fitting t-shirt, and tennis shoes. Jerry looked up at the steely blue eyes staring back at him and asked, "Is Debbie dead?" "No…at least not yet. She is catatonic. The poison I administered is eating away at her brain. Her mind is wasting away, and her body is in such agony that she can no longer communicate. She knows you're here, so feel free to say anything you like to her. She can hear you." Jerry looked at her with cold, yet sad eyes and asked, "Why did you do this to her? She was innocent." The Eagle put a tourniquet on Jerry and slapped his arm hard several times to raise a vein while responding, "No one is innocent. Not you, not Debbie, not me or mankind. Ms. Atwater took lives and assisted in torture. She got what she deserved as you are about to get." Jerry looked over at Deb and said, "Debbie, if you can hear me, the whole mission wasn't a total failure. I got Billy Stone. I fucked him up the ass, and in the end, he got shot by some federal agent."

Debbie didn't react, and Jerry looked at the Eagle as he was setting the IV in his arm and asked, "Why are you killing us? We were the victims. I thought you fought for the victims? Isn't that what the Iron Eagle does?" With the IV line set, the Eagle called out for Sara, who brought him the syringe with the light blue liquid in it. The Eagle stuck the needle into the IV line but before pressing the plunger to kill Pinskey, he looked him in the eye and said, "I defend the innocent. I avenge the wronged. I'm a preventer. I try to stop bad things from happening." The Eagle grabbed his tablet off a table and pulled up the manifesto of Jerry and his friends. He put the tablet in front of him and said, "This manifesto of yours and your late friends speaks of the atrocities that you faced at the hands of the 'pretty people.' If you and your friends had gone after the perpetrators of the crimes against you, you would never have popped up on my radar, and even if you did, knowing the depths of their depravity, I would most likely have helped you. However, you and your friends took it way too far. This document, which none of you ever intended to be read as an explanation for your actions, calls for the mass murder of hundreds of men, women, and children. In a rampage of epic proportions, these people had done you and your friends no wrong. Why should they die?"

Jerry looked on doe-eyed. The Eagle continued, "As I thought, you never considered that there are no innocents in the world, but there are those who don't deserve to be victims for the sake of being victims. Your motives were simple. See how high you could press the body count and get away with it. That's not about avenging a wrong. That's not about punishing the punishers. That's about taking life and death into your own hands and deciding who lives and who dies in an arbitrary fashion. I stopped it, but you're not the only ones planning these things, and I only stopped this one. There are others that I won't be able to stop. I can only hope that in catching and exacting justice on you and your friends that I send a message to other would-be murderers to watch out because they will never know if there's an Iron Eagle waiting for them to make their move, and if so, how much more will he make them suffer."

The Eagle pushed the plunger, and the solution entered Jerry's vein. He howled in agony as the poison worked its way through his body and to his heart. He screamed out to the Eagle, "I hope you suffer a hundred times worse than what you have done to me and Debbie and others." He shuddered and closed his eyes, and the Eagle said, "You will die slowly. May God not have mercy on your soul." Jerry opened his eyes, his face red with anger and pain. He grunted a few times then said, "RIGHT BACK AT YOU, MOTHERFUCKER. RIGHT MOTHERFUCKIN' BACK AT YOU." Jerry threw his head back violently against the table, and his whole body spasmed as the poison took hold. His eyes began to gloss over, and the Eagle took a second syringe of clear liquid and injected it into the IV. "Your doom is set. Enjoy my hell upon you."

Sara had been standing outside the room and heard the conversation between Jerry and the Eagle. When he emerged, she asked, "Do you think that's what's going to happen to you? That you will end up a victim of your own torture?" He shrugged his shoulders and walked into the conference room where Chris lay unconscious. "Can you hand me a shot of stimulant, please?" Sara walked out and came back with the medication and then sat down in one of the meeting chairs in the conference room right below the glowing red eyes of the symbol of the Iron Eagle on the wall behind her. John gave Chris the injection, and it took only seconds, and he was alert.

Chris jerked awake and looked around and saw Sara sitting at the head of a table and above her head was a large wood carving of the Iron Eagle's logo. He let out a sigh and said, "John's the Eagle?" Sara nodded slowly as John sat next to Chris on the couch. Chris looked over at him and said, "You…you. Of all the people in the world, I would never have suspected that you were the Iron Eagle or that you are capable of such brutality." John sat for a moment contemplating Chris's words and then said, "Brutality is brought on by ourselves, an eye for an eye so to speak." "You're a religious nut?" Chris asked, looking at him with confusion. John laughed, stood up, and talked as he walked to Sara.

"I'm not religious at all, Chris. Religion gets in the way of logic. I believe in a deity, though I'm baffled by anyone who would believe in a deity that cared what they believed. I mete out justice within these walls and have been doing so for several years." Chris sat up and asked, "But you weren't always here? You had other locations and other victims going back to your Marine Corps days." John nodded, sitting down next to Sara. He was about to say something else when he spotted Jim standing in the doorway, in his and Sara's line of sight but not Chris's.

"What would you do with the animals I have dealt with over my long career? Locked them up? Put them on trial? Allowed them to parade their atrocities against men, women, and children before the media and the world? Allowed the killers to revel in the publicity machine and inflict more suffering upon the families' victims? Allowed them to take pride and satisfaction in reliving their atrocities again by watching the horror in the faces of the families, as they relived the horror of their loved ones' losses through the eyes of the killer? There is no justice in that, Chris. That is an injustice and an insult to the memory of the victims."

"What if you are killing innocent people?" "Not possible." Chris had a look of arrogance in his face. "And how can you, the Iron Eagle, know beyond a reasonable doubt the guilt of those you kill?" John laughed and so did Jim. Chris looked over to see him walk into the room and sit down next to John and Sara. "Police fuckin' work for one, kid!" Jim said while pulling a cigarette out of his left top pocket and putting it into his mouth. Chris sat silent. Jim motioned to Sara and John for approval, and they nodded.

Jim pulled out his Zippo and lit the cigarette and said, snapping the unit shut, "The Iron Eagle doesn't go around looking for the worst of the worst. Believe it or not, the bulk of the cases he's solved through the years have been on hunches and good research. Do you think he knew about Walter Cruthers, the Basin River Killer, Stewart Roskowski, Simon Barstow, and so many other high profile cases? Fuck no, man… sometimes he got lucky, other times he had detailed research, and he always pays attention. Fuck, Chris, the Eagle saved our country twice, and tonight he saved the lives of hundreds of kids from a massacre of horrendous proportions. Does the Eagle save everyone? Fuck no…how could he? He's not a goddamn super hero. He's a fuckin' man, a well-trained military and police-educated man, battle tested and street smart. You would not even be sitting here if not for John and the Eagle."

Chris asked Jim, "How long have you known?" "From day one, brother, from day fuckin' one." "Who else knows John's the Eagle?" Sara spoke up, "Barbara, Gail Hoffman, Jade, Karen, some of John's close Marine Corps brothers, and now you!" For a long time, he sat looking into the faces in the room. He stood up and asked, "So what now…do you kill me?" John laughed as did Jim and Sara. John said, "I hope not. I want to train you. I want you to work with me and learn how to profile these sick people then find them and eliminate them."

Chris shook his head, "I'm not a murderer, John. I'm sorry, man…you might have your reasons, but they aren't mine. I can't see any situation that would drive me to do the things the Eagle does and has done." John stood and said, "That's why I want to train you, Chris, so you don't have to live the nightmare that I did after becoming the Eagle. If you know who you are out of the shoot, you will be better prepared to protect others." Chris said, "Yet with all of your training, you couldn't save your wife?"

John put his head down, and Sara put her hand on John's arm and shot Chris a short glaring stare and said, "That's a low blow, Chris." John shook his head, looking at Sara who was glaring at Chris. "No, Sara, he's right. You're right. Even with all of my training I could not save Amber. I have played that night and those decisions over and over in my head a million times. I can't change what happened, but I sure as hell learned from it." "Did Steve Hoffman know you were the Eagle?" Chris asked softly. "Yes…in the end." "And what was his reaction?" John laughed under his breath, "A lot like yours. Look, you have to make the decisions on your life and your future. I think you have what it takes to do this type of work, but you have to make the decision." Chris sat down and said, "Look, John, I will keep your secret, that is not to say that I condone what you are doing. It's because I respect you and Jim and the rest of you, and there is some redeeming quality that they see in the Eagle. I don't. I will work for the FBI but don't ask me to get involved in killing people, that's where I draw the line. If I have to kill in the line of duty, so be it, but not as judge, jury, and executioner."

John looked at him and said, "I respect your feelings, and I will not bring the subject up again. Now, you have a flight back to Quantico in the morning and it's late, so how about we call everyone who's free and have dinner before we fly you back tomorrow?" Chris nodded, and the four walked out of the lair and into the main house. Chris looked at John and asked, "Karen knows?" John nodded. "She told me about the Eagle saving her from her adoptive father." John was about to answer when the doorbell rang, and he heard Karen's voice in the entryway. He looked at Chris and said, "Why don't you ask her? I think you will find the story enthralling." Chris said, "I know her story. The darkness of it and the light. I know who saved her but that doesn't change the way I feel." Karen stopped in the doorway and looked at John and Sara then at Chris, "So, you know who John's alter ego is?" Chris nodded and asked, "Why didn't you tell me?" She smiled and said, "It's not my place. If John wants you to know who the Eagle is, he will tell you. I will say that if John has confided his alter ego to you it means he both trusts you and sees in you something of himself."

Chris rejected the whole idea. Karen said softly, "When we look inside ourselves, we discover who we are. If we spend our whole lives looking out, we miss everything." Chris looked at her with confusion and asked, "I don't understand. What the hell does that mean?" Karen laughed, "You will understand soon enough. I just hope it is not at the expense of the life of someone close to you." She asked what was up, and John and Sara told her they were seeking dinner guests. She said, "I'm on board. Would you care to join us, Chris?" He looked on at all of them and said, "Yeah…sure. Why not?"

Jim called Barbara, and she met them all at the house. Jade and Jessica were working the scene in Northridge and had their hands full with several cases and could not break away. As the group sat down for a meal in the formal dining room, Chris asked, "Does your staff know about the Eagle?" John shook his head, and the group sat eating their meal and conversing about the events of the past several days with no more talk of the Eagle.

CHAPTER TWENTY-THREE

The deep web was the source of the weaponry.

The media was abuzz with the thwarted effort of a student plot to wreak havoc on their school and their student body. The press released the details, censored video, and audio confessions of the teachers and students involved. In the days and weeks that followed, there would be much conversation about the plot and who had enabled it. The inventory of ammunition that Tim Elliott had been amassing from overseas that was purportedly coming from his father, Brigadier General Gary Elliott, was not live. The munitions he sent home to his son were deactivated. The deep web was the source of the weaponry that the students had acquired; however, in the end, law enforcement would never be able to nail down exactly who provided it to the boys or trained them to use it. The manifesto, once released by Special Agent John Swenson of the FBI, with many sections redacted for national security purposes, painted a picture of a plot so diabolical in its planning and brutal in its actions that it left parents and teachers across the country in fear for their own schools and fellow classmates.

Swenson released a statement with the manifesto that said, *"This is but the tip of the iceberg to a much larger threat to home and national security."* His hope was to educate and dissuade others from attempting the same type of plot. Sheriff Jim O'Brian praised the efforts of the Iron Eagle for saving hundreds if not thousands of lives. The media ate it up, and the Eagle was in many ways becoming a folk hero in the eyes of the people of Los Angeles. As one reporter put it, *"The city and county of Los Angeles have their own protector, and that protector is the Iron Eagle."*

There was a slight onshore flow coming in off the Pacific Ocean in Malibu, which made for cooler days. The surf was light and John and Sara had just returned from Quantico where Chris Mantel graduated with honors and accepted his first assignment with the Los Angeles field office of the FBI. Jim and Barbara had joined them, as did Karen, on the trip. They all flew back home together while Chris stayed behind to do some last minute packing to prepare for his trip back to LA.

John was leaning on the edge of the infinity pool, looking out over the sea in the late afternoon sun. Sara, Jade, Barbara, and Karen were all sunbathing nude on the deck around the pool, and Jim was reading over an election report of the three finalists for his job. It was mid-September, and in the second to last debates for sheriff of LA County three candidates rose to the top, and he had to decide who to endorse. Two of the three candidates he knew too well; they were both under sheriffs in his department, but he didn't care for either. The first was Tom Kazinski. Jim knew him well but didn't care for the type of police work that he stood for. The second was Danny Hart. Jim liked Danny, but he was a soft touch, and he knew that in the thick of things Hart didn't have what it would take to deal with the big and difficult issues.

Then there was the surprising popularity of Deputy Samantha (Sam) Prichard. She had been in many battles in the department and on the front line through all of the events of the past several years and, in Jim's own words to Barbara, was the perfect candidate to lead the department. She was a diehard cop. If she was cut, she would bleed sheriff's department green. She was a hardnosed, hard drinking and smoking cop who had a nose for trouble and a keen sense of what was going on in the department. Her star was rising, and Jim felt that she would make the perfect successor. He called her up and asked her to meet him for lunch at Santiago's, an invitation she gladly accepted.

Jim had his corner table outside the restaurant, and he sat reading the paper when Sam announced herself. "Sheriff O'Brian, thank you for the invitation." Jim put the paper down and stubbed out the cigarette that he had been smoking and asked her to sit. As she took a seat Jim said, "Please, Sam, call me Jim. I am in my final months as sheriff, and this is an informal meeting." Sam sat down, and Jim offered her a beer. She took it from him and smacked the bottle on the edge of the table and sat back and said, "Thanks, Jim, so what the fuck do you want to meet with me about?" Jim laughed at her candor. Sam stood only five foot three, and she worked very hard to hide her beauty. She was off duty and had come in a pair of black slacks and a tight sweatshirt that showed off her ample breasts. She was in great physical shape, and her long black hair against her natural olive skin and brown eyes made her mysterious and attractive.

Jim said, "You work awful damn hard not to be attractive, Deputy. You should use all of your assets if you want to win this election." Sam took a drink of the beer and said, "I want the people to see a sheriff, Jim, not a fuckin' Victoria Secret's model. I want to be judged like any other candidate…any other male candidate." Jim laughed, opening another beer and said, "Sam, that ship has sailed. Are you intentionally ignoring the press? They started digging everywhere since that debate to find the most provocative photographs they can of you, and they have published quite a few in recent days. You're a good cop; I know that, you know that, the whole goddamn department knows that. So, give up this tough woman crap and run on your record and your plans for the department. Let your fuckin' hair down, disarm these two other fuckers and the media, and you will win this election." Sam sat drinking her beer and asked if she could smoke.

Jim nodded, and she pulled out a cigarette and asked, "Why the sudden interest in me, Jim?" "You finally rose to the top in this race, and I believe that you will make a great Sheriff for Los Angeles County. I know your competition well. They are not sheriff material. They are good at their jobs, but they are not made for what it means to oversee an entire county and city as well as be the ruling power in Los Angeles police work." Sam took a deep drag off her cigarette and asked, "And you think that I am?" "It makes no fuckin' difference if I think you are. Do you think you are? If you're in this race for some women's rights bullshit, then you're in it for all the wrong reasons. Women's rights are protected, and the people of Los Angeles and LA County need to feel protected. What the fuck is your motivation in becoming sheriff?"

"To protect the people of Los Angeles, to protect the rights of all, and to capture the Iron Eagle and end his reign of vigilante justice on this city." Jim was taking a drink of his beer when she was speaking, and he snorted beer out his nose in laughter at the last line of her sentence. He got his composure and said, "Really? Fuckin' really? You want to focus your energy on a ghost who helps us and the people? The Eagle is more popular in LA than the fuckin' president, and you want to focus on bringing him down?" Sam took a drink of her beer and said, "I thought that's what you've been trying to do for pushing two decades. You have had a sudden change of heart?" Jim laughed and said, "Look, Sam, if you're going to run on a platform of catching the Eagle, then you might as well pack it in, that is political suicide. The Iron Eagle is as much a part of law enforcement as we are, so if you're going to tell the people of LA you want to lock him up, you might as well get back in your cruiser and work the streets."

Sam took a hit off her cigarette and reached back and took her hair out of the ponytail it was in and let it fall down around her shoulders. She shook her head hard, and her hair settled on her shoulders and down her back. She lifted her sweatshirt and pulled it off, revealing a tight low-cut red blouse and ample cleavage. She took a drink of her beer and asked, "Is this what you're thinking of when you say 'let my hair down' and 'allow my beauty to sell me into office?'" Jim let out a laugh and said, "Now, you're coming into focus, Sheriff Pritchard; you're coming into focus. How old are you?" "That's an illegal question." "I'm not asking it as your goddamn employer. I am asking it as your endorser and potential voter." "I will be forty in October." "Are you married?" "Divorced...marriage didn't take. My husband couldn't handle a strong woman...and a woman who was a cop." "What skeletons do you have in your closet?" Sam sat back, finishing off the beer and asked, "Before I go down this road with you, are you going to endorse me?" Jim nodded, opening two more beers and handing one to Sam.

"You're goddamn right, I am, and not because you're beautiful, but because you are smart, well-disciplined, and you will make the best sheriff of all the candidates out there." Sam took a swig off the beer and asked, "And if I'm elected, am I going to meet the Iron Eagle?" Jim sat back in his chair, looking out at the sea in the late afternoon sun and said, "The Eagle comes with the job, so I would guess that he will reveal himself in time to you." She stubbed out the cigarette and asked, "Do you know who the Eagle is?" "If you didn't already know the answer to that question, you would not have asked me." The two sat talking late into the afternoon. Jim had his candidate for sheriff, and as they talked, he learned they had a great deal in common, and he commented several times that she was the perfect person for his job.

DARK CANYON

The Iron Eagle Series: Book Ten

PROLOGUE

South Central Los Angeles has always been the hot seat of gang violence for all races and creeds. It had only been escalating in recent years, especially in the wake of the LA fires. Turf wars had turned into literal war, and every ethnic group was fighting for its own share of the city's pie.

It was just after midnight in late September. The lowered Acura two-door sedan with blacked out windows turned the corner of South Vermont onto West 59th Drive. Wilson's Burgers looked more like a prison than a local fast food joint with its barred windows and doors. The burger joint had been in the family for decades and had weathered more than one storm of social unrest. Barry Wilson sat in his Cadillac Escalade with two other young gangbangers waiting for their target.

"You sure you wants to do this, bro?" Arty Molsen asked, holding a fully automatic Uzi in his lap while Anthony Washington sat in the back seat of the car with an AK-47. Barry was holding his own Uzi and said, "It's the only way, bro…dis shit has to stop, and it stops here, man. They're on our turf…what the fuck is up wid dat shit? Mother fuckers…trying to take our shit, man…we has to fight back."

The car turned off its lights as it turned the corner and slowly crept down the street. The street lights had been shot out years ago, and the city gave up on replacing them about the same time. It was pitch black but for a security light over Wilson's Burgers' parking lot. The car kept creeping along in silence past Wilson's and the Escalade, on down the street into the darkness. Bae Hun and Chun Lee were driving extra slow. They knew who their targets were, and they wanted to get the drop on them. Bae asked Chun, "You know where these three are at?" Chun looked at the GPS on the dashboard and said, "Dey here. Dis area. Dat what Han tell me." Bae had a sawed off shotgun in his lap, and Chun had an Uzi. They drove the dark dead end street with no sign of life outside of some bangers hanging out in front of a small house near the end of the street.

Bae pulled into a driveway to turn around and that brought several young men off the stoop and into the street. Several of them had like-colored bandanas tied to their jeans, which rode low on their hips. They all had hand guns tucked into their waistbands, and they stood making gang hand gestures and pointing at the car as Bae moved slowly to pass them. One of the men from the stoop pulled a handgun from his belt and pointed it at the windshield of Bae's car, but he just smiled with the windows up and said, "Try homey…shoot at me car you get surprise!" Chun started laughing and said, "Why not run them down?"

Bae kept driving slowly forward, pushing the guys with the front of his car. "No want to do dat…then we hit and run, bring more war to our hood." The men parted but didn't fire as the windows were blacked out, and they couldn't see inside. Bae got back to the corner and parked near the intersection, and they plugged in the address information again.

Barry saw the Acura this time, and he said, "Dat might be da mother fuckers." The three men stepped out of the vehicle and started to walk across the parking lot toward the car.

The three sharp pops on the roof of the apartment building where Katrina Montrose lived woke her from a sound sleep. She listened for more noise, but it was quiet. She had her phone in her hand ready to call 911. The shooter stood in darkness, looking down at the Escalade and the Acura. He knew the cars well, and he knew that both were armed with bullet-proof glass…he was prepared for that. The shooter had lured Bae and Chun out of hiding with an anonymous tip that their drug lines were about to be cut off, and that their gang would be helpless against the broods gang that controlled the south side. Bae and Chun were the second in command to one of the most violent Korean gangs in LA. The Hun-Sun-Ha gang was known for its sheer brutality. They controlled the streets of Koreatown with an iron fist, and they killed with impunity when needed to prove their superiority. The shooter knew that the two in the Acura were no strangers to this part of the city. They killed here often but not tonight. Tonight, these two and one of the second most violent gangs in LA, Brotherhood United, headed up by Barry Wilson and company, were to be his victims. The shooter set his rocket propelled grenade launcher through the studs of the building across the street and had several rocket heads as well as hand ordnance to wipe out everyone below.

Bae and Chun sat looking at their GPS when they heard banging on the outside of the car. They could see three men with bandanas over their faces banging on the trunk and roof, calling them out. The two men sat in silence as the men beat on the car, and Bae said, "Will need new paint job after this." Chun laughed as gunfire erupted at the car. Barry and Arty started firing at the car from a few feet away, but the bullets were bouncing off the glass and the body without making a dent. "Shit man…dey got fuckin' armor, man!" Arty said before the first rocket struck near the car, exploding and sending all three men flying in pieces through the air. Bae and Chun were dead on impact, and the open driver side of the Acura where the grenade hit looked in on two charred bodies.

The shooter turned his head and then saw a group of about two dozen other Brotherhood gang members running down the street, firing their weapons indiscriminately. Several bullets went through walls, doors, and windows of residences, and there were cries from inside the homes from injured people.

He threw several grenades that blew nearly all of the men to pieces. He picked off three others with a high-powered sniper rifle, and the street went quiet but for the moaning and screaming of the injured. With sounds of police sirens in the distance, he started packing up his equipment and said, "Well, that worked out really, really well. Chalk up another great round of kills." And in silence, he disappeared without being seen or anyone even knowing what had happened.

Jim O'Brian pulled up on the scene within a half hour of the attacks. He saw Jade Morgan off in the distance, throwing out a yellow tarp. He called out to her and asked, "How many fuckin' people we got here, Jade? It looks like a goddamn war zone." Jade yelled back to Jim and said, "Well, if you take into account just blown up body parts, shit, Jim, maybe a hundred." Jim's face sank as he walked up to her. "Jesus, Jim, you look like you saw a ghost." "A hundred people, really?" Jade laughed again and said, "No…ten, maybe twenty total. But the killer blew them to pieces with ordnance, so this crime scene is going to require a bucket and a sponge." Jim let out a half-hearted laugh and asked who else she called. "All the usual suspects, Jim, with a few new ones."

He was about to ask who when he heard Samantha Pritchard call out to him from across the street, "So, what do we have here, Sheriff?"

"A fucked up mess is what we have, Sam. One giant fucked up mess." John pulled up in his Silverado, and he and Chris appeared in front of the headlights. John asked, "Another attack?" Jim and Jade nodded as Sam stood off to the side, looking at John and Chris, not knowing what to say. Jim called out to John and said, "Are you and Agent Mantel going to stand there with your cocks in your hands, or are you going to get your asses in here and help us figure out the scene?"

John and Chris both walked under the crime scene tape as did Sam, and John said, "What's to analyze, Jim? It's the same M.O. as the last two killings. Our killer is using military weapons to kill gangbangers… hell, we should be giving him a gold star for the street cleanup he's doing. Gang violence is down thirty percent in the past two weeks of this guy's reign." Sam looked at John and said, "You're not suggesting, Agent Swenson, that we roll up our investigation and go on about our business and let this guy keep killing?" John was putting on a pair of latex gloves that Jade had thrown at him and Chris as he reached out his huge hand and said, "John Swenson. I don't believe we have been properly introduced. Jim, here, tells me you're a hell of a cop, and that you just got his endorsement for Sheriff of Los Angeles and LA County. Congratulations. What are you doing out on a crime scene at one-thirty in the morning? Shouldn't you be at home in bed getting your beauty rest for campaigning or something?" Chris hit John in the shoulder and said, "Hey, she's a cop, not a politician." John looked over at Chris and said, "Well, I see you two need no introductions."

Sam and Chris looked at each other, and Jim asked, "If you're done playing grab ass, we need to work this scene and look for the note. We know it's not on the ground." John looked around at the buildings and spotted the glint of steel in the ambient light from the security light from Wilson's Burgers. "I got the shooter's position. Chris, follow me. Let's retrieve the note and the rest of the evidence." Sam yelled out after the two men as they headed for the two-story building, "Don't go tromping through our fuckin' crime scene. Take photographs, use your tablets, but don't manhandle things like you did the last time."

Jim let out a laugh and yelled to John, "Who does she fuckin' remind you of, dickhead?" John and Chris were able to enter the building and get to the roof. They found the grenade launcher stand as well as two used rocket covers and a sealed note in clear plastic. John called down to Jim and said, "Same shooter, same M.O. We have a list of who he killed and what they did to deserve it." John and Chris processed the rooftop scene and then walked back down to greet them.

Jade looked on and said, "The same dude, huh?" John nodded, and Jim said, "Great. We have another nut job on the loose…another vigilante who wants to kill gang members." Sam looked at John with the note in his gloved hand and said, "I don't think so…yeah…this guy wants these gangbanger thugs dead, but I'm not buying that this is some random guy who wants to clean up the streets." John smiled and handed the note to Jim who read it over quickly and then handed it back to him. Jade handed John an empty evidence bag and said, "For God's sake, on the off chance that we catch the fucker doing this, have a chain of custody, so the damn evidence does not get thrown out at trial."

Sam smarted off and said, "Trial? What trial? If this isn't the Iron Eagle doing the killing, I'm sure he's looking for the fucker, and if he gets him, we will see his confession in HD video as he's being killed. Ain't that right, Jim?" Jim just laughed and said, "Let's wrap this up, folks. I want to get some sleep before the sun rises on another day in the hell that is my career." Jim looked at Sam and said, "I checked out your numbers, and you're way ahead in the polls. With any luck, in a few short months you get to take over this shit while I retire to a beach somewhere." Jim looked at John and asked, "I am going to live long enough to die naked and drunk with Barbara on some beach somewhere, right?" John shrugged his shoulders as everyone around laughed.

About the Author

Roy A Teel Jr. is the author of several books, both nonfiction and fiction. He became disabled due to Progressive Multiple Sclerosis in 2011 and lives in Lake Arrowhead, CA with his wife, Tracy, their tabby cat, Oscar, and their Springer Spaniel, Sandy.

CPSIA information can be obtained at www.ICGtesting.com
Printed in the USA
BVOW05*1943070415

395144BV00001B/1/P